The Scale of Maps

The Scale of Maps

Belén Gopegui

Translated by Mark Schafer

City Lights Books Y San Francisco

First published in Spain with the title *La escala de los mapas* (Anagrama, 1993)

First published in the United States of America in 2010 by City Lights Books

Copyright © 1993 by Belén Gopegui

English translation © 2010 by Mark Schafer

All Rights Reserved

Cover and interior book design by Linda Ronan

masscultural council.org

This translation was supported in part by grants from the Arlington Cultural Council, a local agency supported by the Massachusetts Cultural Council, and by the Spanish Ministry of Culture.

Thanks to Professor Alan Smith for introducing me to Belén Gopegui's novel and to Trudy Balch, Dick Cluster and Cola Franzen for their generous feedback on an earlier draft of this translation. Thanks to the Writers' Room of Boston, the (nameless) Boston-area literary translators group, the Arlington Arts Council, and the Spanish Ministry of Culture for their support of this translation, from start to finish.

Library of Congress Cataloging-in-Publication Data
Gopegui, Belén, 1963-
[Escala de los mapas. English]
The scale of maps / Belen Gopegui ; translated by Mark Schafer.
    p. cm.
Translation from Spanish.
ISBN 978-0-87286-510-5
1. Gopegui, Belén, 1963—Translations into English. I. Schafer, Mark.
PQ6657.O65E8313 2010
863'.64—dc22
                    2010038348

Visit our website: www.citylights.com

City Lights Books are published at the City Lights Bookstore,
261 Columbus Avenue, San Francisco, CA 94133

In memory of Miriam

1

If a small man were to kiss your hand then immediately launch into a description of the hand crank used to open a window, what would you do? Given my line of work, I should not have been considering such questions. And yet, I confess that for the first few minutes Sergio Prim had me confused. Standing before me, he spoke of the small metal part. His deep, trembling, porous voice flowed more slowly than was typical in this type of patient. He was considerably shorter than I, and his arms moved about through a lower layer of the air, which perhaps is why I barely noticed them. But memory now highlights the way his hands fluttered like a bashful magician's as the only dissonant note in Mr. Prim's calm presence.

"Facing my desk is a window that overlooks an inner courtyard," he said confidentially. "It's very old: a wooden frame, a black window catch and a pane of frosted yellow glass. You open the catch by turning a crank that is round at the end—let's call it a thick point. I'm asking you for help because I'm considering going to live there."

I led Mr. Prim into my office. The sky had grown dark as if it were about to rain. Sergio discreetly cleared his throat and settled into one of the large armchairs I had inherited from my grandparents. I turned on a table lamp on the other side of the room; its circle of light did not extend to where we sat. Before retreating behind my large wooden desk, I offered him a cigarette, which he declined.

"So, you're considering going to live in your office?"

He gave me a melancholy smile.

"No, not at all. It's not the office that's important but the crank. Though in any case the crank is just one option. There are many points—hollows. If you have no objections let's call them hollows. You're going to tell me that there's nothing wrong with frequenting a few hollows now and then. You're right, quite right. But as you will see"—Sergio Prim's arm fell against the armchair with surprising force—"my problem is that I need them. They are the only way I have to stop myself. This very afternoon, had it not been for a hollow, I certainly would not have made it here, I wouldn't be talking with you now, for I would have snapped the headphones of that boy in the minibus right in two."

I sat up and shuffled a few pieces of paper as I attempted to disguise my excitement. Many years back, Julio Bernardo Silveria had come to my office complaining of a similar ailment. His case changed the direction of my doctoral dissertation as well as the biography of my emotions.

"I happened to sit," Prim continued, "directly behind a young man wearing one of those tiny devices for listening to music in private. It was ridiculous. The headset was letting out enough noise—modern, monotonous, you know the kind—to annoy the passengers sitting next to him but not enough for us to enjoy the music naturally. Meanwhile, the young man, oblivious to the racket he was making, was nodding his head as he flipped through the pages of a glossy magazine. I was thinking of Brezo and that irritating little noise only annoyed me more. That was when a small, wicked fantasy came to me. I imagined myself gently grasping each end of that young man's halo and spreading them farther and farther apart until they formed a straight line and—crack!—a broken set of headphones."

"But you restrained yourself," I noted with feigned detachment.

"Not exactly. I looked for a hollow. I found it in the fabric of the coat the man sitting next to me was wearing. And I inhabited that nook for the remainder of the trip. Look, nook. As you can see, one letter can alter a man's entire life."

Prim slid the armchair closer and as he leaned forward his figure gathered strength. He had the type of build that favors its owner when he is sitting, preferably behind something that conceals his disproportionate stature. Two short lines connected his neck to his shoulders. His face, on the other hand, seemed to have been molded by a cruel twist of fate to sit atop the uniform of an elegant messenger for the czar: the eyes of a startled fox, a straight nose, cheeks the shape of equilateral triangles, a head of thick dark curls, and under the shadow of an ample gray moustache flecked with white, his lips, shiny and red like a wax apple.

"Perhaps you would like to know why I chose the fabric of a coat," he added softly. "I can't answer that yet. As far as I have determined, objects conceal invisible hollows. But I don't yet know if our ability to detect them depends on a common characteristic—if all objects are interconnected—or on the state of the person who approaches them seeking protection. What I do know is that I've started to write a treatise on the subject."

"It's an interesting idea," I said by way of encouragement. More than once at the beginning of my career, I had the misfortune of seeing how a hasty judgment, a hint of indifference or scorn could irremediably demolish men who held childlike illusions. Ever since, I have taken special care not to discourage patients who choose to take on tasks of their own free will. In this case, however, my interest was disingenuous, like that of a photographer taking a picture of the bullet that will kill him.

Sergio Prim settled into the armchair and gazed at a corner of the ceiling. From where he sat, a distant tone in his voice, he reprimanded me:

"It's not that easy. Do you know that the first known *mappa mundi*, made by Anaximander of Miletus, dates to the sixth century before Christ? There was a time, exaggerated and self-absorbed, when our planet existed without maps. If a man wished to represent a region of Africa on a flat surface, he had to go there or else rely on the reports, memoirs, and accounts brought back by explorers. I find myself in the same situation. To write a treatise on the hollow—all points belong to a single hollow—I have to go there. It still has not been mapped, and the few eyewitness reports by those who claim to have frequented it are terribly imprecise. Thus my 'interesting idea,'" he said, repeating my words with a look of reproach, "requires that I set out on an expedition, that at the age of thirty-nine, I go off in pursuit of an unknown dwelling place. Do you see what I'm saying? To venture into as yet undiscovered regions with this feeble body of mine. And don't think I use that last adjective lightly. Over the course of my life, I have broken my femur three times, my ulna twice, and my metatarsus once. My muscles often tremble inexplicably, I experience dizzy spells and feel that I'm on the verge of crumbling into the air."

As if trying to demonstrate this, Sergio Prim began wrestling with his dark overcoat. Underneath was a wool sweater of a color somewhere between beige and pink, and the collar of a blue shirt peeked out at his neck. In fact, Sergio Prim was slight of build in the torso if not exactly skinny. Yet his words, combined with the smartness of his attire—the straight crease in his pants, the refined, creamy weave of his sweater—made me imagine that his body was fragile, thin as a sheet of paper, practically fictitious.

"What is the reason for your visit, Mr. Prim?" I asked, secretly afraid that the business about the hollow would be nothing but a fleeting obsession.

"I want to know what's going to happen with Brezo, the Vanished Woman," he said slowly. "For a week now her eyes have been flying around like bats, knocking against the walls, spinning round and round on the blades of imaginary fans in every room of my apartment."

Sergio Prim went over to the window. When he opened it, the moiré curtains fluttered in the wind and the lamp shook. It had started to rain. I paused for two or three minutes, listening to the slow drizzle. But Prim interrupted me:

"By the way, did I mention that I'm being followed?"

His remark startled me. Perhaps he was one of those people who spend their days reading books on psychiatry, write down symptoms in a notebook, study them, and then come in to harass us. Once my beloved had sent just such a person to spy on me. I observed Sergio Prim with suspicion. His light sweater blended with the cheek-colored fabric of the curtains. He stood with his back to me, looking out at the street, his prominent head round and nocturnal. Then he closed the window and I saw his face reflected in the glass. I relaxed. Sergio Prim had a sober look on his face and was not lying.

Sergio Prim was not lying because I am Sergio Prim.

2

Never before have I revealed my strategies. I am embarrassed. I wish I could expunge myself with an eraser while you, readers, grasp the nature of my ruse.

Only to reappear in the next paragraph. I was always a prudent man. I would offer thanks for that which did not deserve gratitude and beg forgiveness for actions that could not possibly have caused offense. So I don't mind doing it again: Please forgive me, or at least accept my explanation. What would you have thought as you read these pages had I started by saying, "My first visit to the psychologist took place . . ."? You might not agree with my conclusions, but you would be mistaken to dismiss them simply because I, their architect, am unbalanced. No, no, not at all. I was engaged in a project in which the psychologist played a role, and that is why I went to see her. She would provide me with the scientific foundation, the touchstone or black siliceous rock against which I would rub the gold of my imagination. Over the last three days, however, events have accelerated, and I have come to rest at this Earthly convergence of crosshairs, a place free of error whose image weighs on me like a debt of honor, like a final responsibility. It is eight in the evening. Outside, the willows yield to the shadows with a shiver. In the living room below someone puts on a record of *habaneras*; the music filters through the hallways. I wrap a scarf around my neck, open the window, exhale her name—"Brezo"—and let it float in the air like an iridescent ring of smoke.

I stand here before you, I, the hopeless substitute for the strategic genius who should have been carrying out this mission, preparing to deploy my troops with the exquisite fervor of someone who knows that winning or losing is out of his hands. In a hotel room, on an unfamiliar table, I will draw the maps and give the final orders to an exiled band of guerrillas in rebellion that is none other than myself. Oh, Brezo Provocateur. Why do you incite my outlandish imagination, incite it and me, the two of us, to climb over barricades when we are not agile, to suffer insults and fight duels when we are not bold?

Watch how I found Brezo in a supposition. It was night-time and it was raining. The red brake lights, white headlights, and orange directionals created a ballet of shifting reflections on the pavement. It was October, but my head filled with strings of lights and trees lit up like Madrid at Christmas. Immediately I thought "Maybe she's back," because every year, no matter where she was, Brezo would return to spend Christmas Eve with her widower father. I imagined her walking from her house on Calle Alcalá and imagined her recognizing my silhouette under the eaves of the bus shelter. "Let's suppose," I said to myself, "that I felt her cold, slender fingers covering my eyes. What would I do?" At that moment the number 9 opened its doors and Brezo appeared. She got off the bus escorted by a cluster of passengers. I watched as she quickly crossed the street, the walk signal blinking, and I debated with myself, frozen, astonished, as if trapped and suspended within a single, gigantic, accented "o," the accent as large as it was terrifying. Traffic was moving again when I snapped out of this trance, but I took off running, entrusting myself to that little red man, and reached the sidewalk on the other side of the street safe and sound. I ran uphill, such a large, grotesque figure—at my age!—the shoes of a duck slapping the puddles, my left arm raised, umbrella at the ready. I ran disheveled by my urgency until I could almost touch her, and I would have covered her eyes with my hands had she not turned around first.

"Sergio Prim!" you laughed, my devilish geographer with walnut-colored eyes.

"Brezo Varela," I stammered as you took shelter under my umbrella and wrapped your arm around mine. "Brezo," and I held back from saying, "Perch beneath this portable porch."

Four unimaginable months have passed. Do you see that bicycle without brakes speeding down that sandy path? Do you see the gentleman steering it in terror, hands over his ears, legs crossed, his torso bouncing on the seat? If you get a little closer you will recognize my face. And I confess to you that on that night, walking arm in arm with Brezo, all I could do was to make sure the brakes were not going to work.

A man takes a step and nothing happens. A man crosses the threshold of the same doorway 14,637 days in a row. And the 14,638th time he discovers a stag with a full rack of antlers under the lintel. For ten years now I've seen Brezo only during vacations, listening—I, her listener, I, her mentor—to stories of her life, offering her made-up episodes from my own. Why bore her with the truth? As you may have guessed, the story of Brezo and me is none other than that of the stag. Listen. A man walks alone until he no longer has the faintest notion of the number that denotes his loneliness. Night falls and the same man is walking arm in arm with the woman he loves. She lifts her head, looks at him, then takes his hand in hers, laughs. And the man doesn't know what to do. You'll tell him: Kiss her. Of course, kiss her, but sex is transient, ladies and gentlemen, passion is chancy. Who am I to offer shelter to the body of another? And yet, I kissed her.

Brezo came up to my apartment, looked out from the balcony, and let me stroke her on the side like a bird. It was not yet nine o'clock. The twilight of neon signs filled my room. I got undressed first, and she was meek and beautiful as she took off her white shirt. To watch her shoulders, the agility with which she moved, acquired in unnamed experiences. Slender and proportioned, she lay on the bed naked, as if wishing to be my own representation—not Brezo, not her life story, just a representation offered up to me, her arms extending the lines of her body, my hand on her back, and my astonishment. Why had she chosen me? Why, after all these years? I am a small man, I have the shoulders of an old boxer, and pale skin. To look at her was to perceive a total absence of silences, as if it were at last possible to imagine a space without crouching monsters, without painful memories, as if I had lost my fear of tripping on the crack between two tiles, of plunging my hand between one section of air and another.

I caressed her slowly. At first she was afraid of being overtaken by ecstasy, so I protected her. I asked her before I made any unusual movement and took care to rouse a gentle purring in her body until I watched her wake fully to desire, lifting herself like an apparition over my misplaced body, my dazzled eyes, and she existed in me. I filled her and she responded with a moan like a bubble of light and an ecstatic smile. My god—what had caused taciturn Brezo, somber Brezo, self-absorbed and serious Brezo to smile at me like that? My hands dreamed over her small breasts, I kissed her in disbelief, defenseless in the face of her defenselessness, which she offered to me, yet growing larger like a happy man. All the while her back was time itself, and years of my life rippled through her thighs, years I'd never known, years when I wasn't walking along the fence that surrounded the high school field, quiet and deep in thought, years when no one muzzled my desire, rather, every action I took could always be taken back, for it was beautiful, good, and pleasant. The whites of her eyes so close they were surprised to find me so close. So close that her collarbone fit in my hand, so close that her hair was losing control—enveloping me as I kissed her until she lay fully extended, the plain of a woman. I continue to watch her. Her red nipples are an alarm calling me; she has spilled her sensuality onto my bed for her own amusement. But if I am a skeptic, if I have established solitude as my safe-conduct, what happened to me as I looked at her face, beautifully distant on account of my body? I was her distance and she was inhabiting me when I heard her say, laughter spilling from her mouth, I feel faint. What did you do to me, madwoman? What are you doing to me?

When she left, day breaking, vain and dissolute, when the white taxi disappeared, I instinctively searched for the smell of Brezo on my clothes. Dumbfounded, I scanned the sidewalk, muttering "I never would have thought. . . ." Finally I ducked into an English pub. As I recovered my senses, I was once again filled with anxiety. I asked for a glass of aged rum, though I rarely drink and even less often do I find myself in frothy spots like this—red leather seats studded with buttons, thick cardboard coasters. It was not Brezo's absence that troubled me but my fear. What would I do with her now? How would I proceed from one day to the next? I never cultivated the art of being with other people. I never learned to reconcile my state of rest, my private convalescence in a lodging room of the world lit by a single lamp, with the sharp breath, like a gust from a storm, that the new guest lets out upon arrival. During that time in my life when I was surrounded by other people—first my family, then Lucía, my wife for four years—I found that people who had just come into the house inevitably spoke in an overly high-pitched voice and stood in the entranceway longer than necessary, squandering words, repeating a message that I in my intolerance meticulously screened out. Moreover, the bodies that had just come in from outside usually brought with them clouds of cold or muggy air, pollen or rain, depending on the season. I would gaze at them from where I sat, submerged in my armchair, and though I've never worn glasses I would feel like a retired professor, one of those professors who connect with the universe through two round, silvery lenses.

I noticed my eyes were burning: I was surrounded by smokers. A young man in a waiter's outfit began to play the piano. A blonde woman with gloves on raked the lapel of a gentleman who looked like me. Get out, I told myself. Get out of here. You can fall asleep tomorrow and you have to finish writing those pages on the southwest sector. Such humidity outside. Such smell of Brezo. Such insomnia filling my apartment.

I hadn't even hung my coat on the office coat rack when the assistant manager, a black-eyed, stately matron, came to pick up my report.

"It's October fourth," she said with oriental inscrutability. I glanced at the date and saw that it was October third. All the time we have left, Brezo, we've been granted so much time.

"Good morning, Mrs. Morales," I replied, concerned. "I apologize for the delay. As you know, we've had problems with the Committee. But I'll have it for you within the hour."

At ten of ten, Brezo called. At nine of ten, a somber Sergio Prim appeared, spurred on by his haste. I couldn't link that voice on the phone with the defenseless body that had brought mine to life the night before. All I heard were words, interference. I can't talk right now. I'll call you later, Brezo-interference.

I barely had time to read through to the last page. I found Elena Morales stirring a cup of coffee she had brewed in her personal coffeemaker. She invited me to pour myself a cup. As she flipped through my treatment of the maps, I tried to figure out the best way to hold the plastic cup without burning my fingers or spilling the coffee. Doña Elena appeared to be satisfied, but one of her feet pulsed beneath her desk. I started to get nervous. Perhaps if I sat down I wouldn't be able to see it any longer. And what should I do with the cup—that blessed cup? Circumstances always get the better of me. I completely understand those admirals who never manage to engage a single ship in battle, who fight the elements their whole lives long. Instead of looking doña Elena in the eye, rather than preparing a short speech concerning the work I'd done, I was fighting with a tiny cup. Elena Morales's shoe stopped moving.

"A fine job," she said and made a vague gesture of approval. I sat there in silence. Two hundred and twenty-four hours of work—not to mention a few additional, unaccounted-for hours—trickled down the drain of that gesture.

"Have they made copies of it yet?"

I nodded meekly, gripping my little cup. The report would serve to thicken the purportedly indispensable annals of bureaucracy. Once incorporated into the project report it would call into question the design of that sector. Considering the small margin we had for maneuvering, the influence my report would have would be infinitesimal, like writing a decimal point, a small decimal point that, in the hands of another geographer, would have been reasonably solid and thick. But where had my vanity gone? Who hasn't needed to feel admiration, applause, warmth—yes, warmth—from his boss? Secretly I begged for a sign, a shaking of hands, a comment whose complicity would justify those three long, headache-filled weeks. Two women I didn't know came in and began to speak with Elena Morales. Sergio Prim slipped out with characteristic discretion.

Back at my desk, the little cup tossed against the side of the wastebasket, I remembered Brezo-bird. I longed to call her but her looming figure rattled me. I was afraid she might sweep me away, though perhaps I was more afraid of denying her three times, that before the cock crowed I would see her three times and three times would fail to feel the giddy unreality that her body had produced in me. When I finally spoke with her she asked me to meet her in the archives of the Naval Museum. I spent the rest of the morning correcting the results of an error in scale in an impact study on how to place a space station in the foothills of the Parque Monfragüe without disturbing the surroundings. How might a woman with ideas of her own be placed in my discreet life in such a way that both of us would come out unscathed? For Brezo was a woman with ideas, outlandish and particular, all her own. Brezo was crazy. I found this out even before I had entered into a friendship with her. I learned this the day I heard her get excited for the first time, ten years ago, in the house where we would meet to work in teams. We had gone out on the balcony to relax for a bit. I was pretending to look at the cars—we were on the twenty-fourth floor—when, amidst the laughter and conversation, I heard the voice of a woman passionately defending Zelinsky's propositions—the American to blame for such unabashedly pretentious phrases as "the geographer should be the architect of utopias"—quoting whole paragraphs from his first manifesto published in *Antipode*, a rusty magazine of radical geography: "Geographical studies can contribute to the destruction of the system"—what system, for god's sake? What system?—"not only through the diagnosis of sociospatial inequalities, but also by providing the tools for correcting them in revolutionary fashion." I turned to look at the woman speaking and was astonished by what I saw: a skinny woman with big eyes that made her look happy, and despite her feverish tone, my impression of her as she leaned backwards over the vertiginous railing was that of a gentle soul. Instead of the severe girl wrapped in brown sackcloth one might have expected to be giving that speech, there you were, conscious of how attractive your body was, decked out in a long sweater and a nearly invisible short skirt. Your low-heeled shoes charted a course toward your knees, which were covered by black stockings. I imagined the backs of your knees. And I must have wondered where your fault was hiding, your divine ailment, your defect, your cross, as my mother would have said. For experience tells me that one must either be defective or have a penchant for imbuing abstractions with so much passion. And so many years later, nestled in my arms, what were you looking for? I remembered my fears of the previous night. "The problem is afterward," I had predicted in silence as you took off your clothes. Nevertheless, "afterward" you raked your fingers lightly across my chest, your eyes sparkling, your knees pressed together.

Brezo, Brezo, to cross over with you I must find a drawbridge suspended somewhere between two worlds: the world of nakedness and that other one, Sergio Prim thought to himself as he walked to the museum. I arrived half an hour before it closed. Only four or five desk lights remained lit in the library. Hunched like insects, several people of questionable appearance were flipping through catalog cards, sharpening impromptu pencils, and filling the metallic receptacle that, instead of cigarette butts, held disturbing colored shavings. You were in the last cubby, but you had already stood up and were walking toward me.

Even though you wore dark clothes, you looked radiant. You asked me to wait ten minutes: you had to consult one more map. So I watched you from the railing. You looked like an insect too, an eye-catching bluebottle fly with an amber head, sipping from sheets of paper. I imagined myself passing through the aura of your skin in the lamplight. Oh, rude dissonance: the feet of a chair scraping the floor. A pencil smoker got up. I watched him walk over to your desk, holding a sheaf of papers like a tray. And there the two of you savored your centennial nectar. The pencil smoker was pointing somewhere with his right hand while his left hand rested on your shoulder. No, it was not jealousy I felt but a sudden helplessness. I envied the ease with which that archivophile placed his hand. Surely he belonged to that fortunate group of people who swing from one body to the next as they move through the world. They use shoulders or waists as handholds, and this is how they counter the lack of balance congenital to our species. Not I: I was not bestowed with the talent to make one affectionate gesture after another, properly chosen so as not to seem hesitant or forced in the least. My hand is always wandering and retreating before it might touch someone's elbow, back, or hip. I am a retreating pair of hands, a body in retreat, alone in the bustle of bodies because I was never taught to kiss people's cheeks or clutch their forearms. I do not know how to let myself go, not even in my desire, not even as I disappear inside you. I enter desire and maybe I find a place to rest, but right away a luminous fence lights up, a flashing orange blaze that compels me to cross, to run.

The pencil smoker returned to his seat, and I began searching through the card catalogs. I had remembered a small discovery from my days as a bookworm and wanted to show it to you. And I wanted to lean over you until my chin rested on your head. I submitted my request and they brought it to me. I let one of my hands alight on the curve of your neck. My sternum, my skeleton trembled, Brezo, as I grazed the lobe of your ear with my thumb.

"Look," I whispered. "The first known illustration of the margeen."

"The what?"

"The margeen, the lost number. They discovered it in Cádiz. They think it dates to the sixteenth century."

A beadle entered with the feet of frightened doves, and the five chairs creaked out of turn. The smokers, you included—please excuse me for a moment, as if time could be forgiven—disappeared behind the large sliding door, their borrowed materials in hand. One by one you returned and began your miniature liturgy: elastic bands snapping against folders, caps clicking onto markers. You were the last to leave, Brezo, because you had spread hundreds of pieces of paper across the table, but also because while you sorted them into mysterious piles, you were asking about the margeen. You are familiar with it now, but my interlocutors may not be. It is said, my friends, that a number located between seven and eight lost with the writings of Diophantus, the algebraist. Of course this is a legend, but I do not have to remind you of the theory that there can be no sign without a referent. It is tempting indeed. Imagine, my friends: another number, an hour every day outside the flow of time, a month unaccounted for every year between July and August. "Where do you come up with these outlandish ideas?" you asked me. Outlandish ideas? They are signals. I signaled to you and now I have become my very own signals, Brezo, perturber of my life. Love does not sweep us away, it pushes us toward the place where, alone, we approach each other in fear.

It rains, the minutes pass, red as the wine I am drinking to stupefy my heart. I wonder if I should speak to confident Brezo, so very lost, or if instead I should address you, my readers with your mute eyes and your archivists' hearts, the final guardians of my discovery. Just know that as she was leaving the museum, Brezo said she was worn out, hailed a taxi, and suggested we go to my apartment. A radio program about how to care for cacti filled the air and neither of us put up a fight. Brezo was falling asleep. I was regretting having agreed to her suggestion: it upset my plans. Sergio was hoping that we might seal a pact that night and preferred neutral territory in which to play his hand: surrounded by strangers who would have impeded bodies from moving toward one another. My first move would be to retreat, playing by the book, and say, "Listen to me, madwoman, girl who caresses coffee cups as if they were cats and a man as if he were an ensemble of musicians, listen: I have lost all my momentum. The years have passed and I have settled into my solitude. I live like that small, autarchical country offered as an example in high school. I am Albania. My natural climate is temperate, it is composed of scraps of unsanitary plains, rugged plateaus, and a collection of abrupt mountains. In my republic, we practice the autarchy of retreat: production for the purpose of self-sufficiency and to protect ourselves from foreign influence. Because living with others is war and devastates me, I have chosen to surround myself with a diffuse constellation of relationships. Their lights are distant and though they barely provide any illumination, they don't cause me much harm either. I practically live in the dark. I live in my brief house, in my brief bed, with brief glimpses of the outside world. And I cannot build up my hopes, for I am a skeptic."

A woman from Málaga wanted to know why the blue flowers on her cactus had withered. While rubbing Brezo's hand to wake her up, I pointed the taxi driver to my door.

6

Using a cup of tea as a ruse, I got Brezo to sit at the table and curb her growing desire to lean on me. She was exhausted. Her slender shoulders swayed, begged to be held in check. I stood my ground and spoke to her of Albania. I even showed her a worn copy of *Reality and Desire*, with a yellowed slip of paper that served as a bookmark peeking out at page 247. Puzzled, she opened the book. I asked her to read the poem titled "Without": "The soul in harmony, alone / desires to live beside the beloved, / with the silence of a rose / blooming on its branch. / The soul in discord, alone / must die beside what is strange, / with the silence of a rose / dropping its petals on its stem." It was of no use. Brezo was blooming and dropping her petals on my desert island. Brezo believed. I, on the other hand, knew what I could trust. I knew that passion is chancy, though I had no idea what fluke had provoked the terrifying sweetness in her eyes when she looked at me—as terrifying as it was unbearable. I knew that reality pits us against one another, that any object subjected to external forces becomes fatigued and deformed. I knew that adoration, subjected to unhappiness, to time, never lasts.

I knew that Brezo adored me. She brought her lips close

to mine, and before I knew it, she was hurling herself naked on top of me. I told myself that the metamorphosis would soon be unleashed. I told myself that a man can make love to a sheet of rain, to a dragonfly, to an acacia. For a second I hesitated: What would happen if I surrendered? One morning the criminal that the police have been hunting for gets up quite serenely, ties his tie with panache, puts on his cufflinks, dials a number, and whispers, "Look for him at eleven-thirty. He will be on Calle X, unarmed and wearing a navy blue suit." But it was utterly futile. When the fugitive surrenders he dissolves, and another person, not a fugitive, takes his place. Sergio Prim must not be hopeful. I ran my finger ever so slowly along Brezo's collarbone and suggested that we go out for dinner.

We made our way through the narrow streets of my neighborhood until we came to Plaza San Ildefonso. It is a rectangle bordered by tall, old houses with patches of light in the windows, wobbly benches, cats in the bushes. Water never pours from the stone spiral in the center. On the southern side is a bar with wooden tables where we used to meet when we were students at the university. Brezo did not yet have the long hair that would eventually hover above her shoulders, suspended as if an impossible cleft of air lay between her shoulders and everything else. Her hair was short, with straw-colored tufts shooting out like small flames that she would shake furiously whenever we argued. Back then we argued all the time. I am nine years older than she is. My general lack of direction led me to the School of Architecture, but it took me two years to pass the first-year exam. I needed to pass two others to get through the third year. I left in my fourth year without finishing, did my military service in Ceuta.

When I started studying geography, I was already feeling old and, like a man who resigns himself to his one and only vice, had grown fond of what I would call the prayer book of evasion. In my notes, which I would occasionally lend to Brezo, I liked to make tiny drawings of things that vanished: the eyelid, keeper of darkness; exhaust pipes; umbrellas; eyeglass cases that get misplaced; the hole in a flat tire through which the air escaped; the phrase exit right, half an actor's body as he leaves the stage. Brezo countered with pragmatic theses: "If you actually left, if one day you really did it. . . ." she would say to me. "The problem with escape artists is that they never actually escape."

Sitting at what was once our table, facing a Brezo who burned like a holiday torch, I launched my attack with the weapons of bygone days.

"Brezo," I said, "what I want is to slip away."

"Still?" she asked, a perplexed look on her face.

"Yes," I said, nodding emphatically. In a gloomy voice, I recalled my final years of high school when I attempted to hide from everyone. I would walk around alone at recess until I heard a voice call out, "Hey, you! Yeah, I'm talking to you!" I wouldn't respond. "Houdini!" and I'd turn around. I, the escape artist, see the short boy with mussed hair crammed into a spacesuit, the teenager tilting his inverted fishbowl in turmoil as if he hadn't heard a thing or even had the faintest idea of his latitude. "So what if I don't know my latitude?" the little boy argues, removing the helmet from his head, offended. "Who cares?"

"My sentiments exactly," I explain to her. "Who cares?"

"You'd rather not know where you are?" she asked, pressing her tongue against her teeth.

"In a manner of speaking."

They had brought us the house soup. Brezo was moving the

saltshaker and lining up the silverware as if they were writing implements on a desk rather than the utensils one might use to eat.

"All right," she said. "You set the rules."

"It's not so much a question of rules as it is of scales."

"Scales?"

"You know that scales do not belong just to geographers. In fact, the entire world uses scales to interpret data. The other day I was in the kitchen and I heard a low rumble through the patio window. It could have been a coffeemaker in one of the apartments, the coffee rising, or an airplane. The sound would have been identical. It's just a matter of scale."

She conceded sleepily.

"Brezo, I'm a small man, but I have the feeling that you picture me within an even smaller scale, which makes me appear quite large. Couldn't you shift scales? Couldn't you enlarge your scale until, in your memory, I was the point that designates a town on a tiny map, the microscopic replica of a blurry, distant, nearly nonexistent Sergio Prim?"

Brezo yawned. She hung her head, chin in her hand. Her elbow was slipping toward one corner of the table.

7

Swift Moccasin, Black Elk, Son of Thunder—that is what the Indians were called in the movies. Throughout the month of October, Brezo had an Indian name as well: it was Love Without a Perch. She flew around me like a woodpecker, pecking small occasional holes, visits and phone calls that laid waste to my day, introducing another's time into my own and leaving me bewildered. It was love without a perch that was taking hold of my gestures, leaving its marks on my hands—which I always kept soft, freshly washed in case she arrived unexpectedly at my house and I were to touch the inside of her—leaving a residue of sadness in the corners of my eyes, the noble halo of tubercular men of old that was Brezo, that mauve and pink circle that was Brezo, that was knowing I would have to love her outside every window frame, outside of time, and at times, outside Brezo herself, like an adulterer, like a sick man who knows the signs of his illness yet hasn't breathed a word of it to anyone. I wasn't about to die, my body was not condemned, but my love was without a doubt. A man cannot raise his love into the sky for more than a few months, yet how does one let her know without causing her any harm, holding back the days, staggering the times we would see each another to prolong the calculation.

At first I was scared of Brezo's presence. Later I learned that I should be scared of her imagination. "At times I imagine you," she told me one afternoon, and I grew dizzy. She had been in my house and had preserved in her memory the location of every object. Then she imagined me. What a way of possessing things. When night fell, for example, I was making my dinner (sliced bread and tuna fish in oil, a tomato, a beer) when suddenly, the plate on the coffee table, the napkin on my knees, the sandwich on its way to my mouth, I thought, "Might she be imagining me?" A few days later it got more complicated: "Might she be imagining that I am wondering whether she is imagining that I . . . ?"

8

Brezo had returned to Spain to apply for an extension of her grant in Helsinki where she was developing an equitable, eco-integrated regional model to be tested in the archipelago of the Baltic Sea. If she didn't get the extension she would have no choice but to finish the project from Madrid. I knew she was worried; her desire to go back would manifest itself, impulsive and urgent, as if she had developed a bond of need or nourishment with Finland. But at other times Brezo fantasized about possibly staying here. Determined to maintain a discreet distance, I never offered her my opinion, not even when she asked for it. "Discretion is a form of cowardice," she declared one morning, and that prelude to a reproach saddened me. We were in the hotel bar, quite close to the northern train station, sitting at the table in the most dimly lit corner of the locale. When she saw the serious look on my face, Brezo-conjurer squeezed the latches on her father's old leather briefcase and took out a gray package.

I opened it with the impatience of a timid man. I was able to remove the string but when I tried to peel off the tape, I tore the paper, revealing an elegant cardboard box with a modern black train drawn against a red background. In the middle a white label read: "Accessory 127. Open-air platform with figures." I looked at her in astonishment. It is, I can now confess, the only useless posses-sion that accompanies me in this White Russian exile from which I write. I keep it in the table drawer. I know that if I were to pick it up for sentimental reasons, I would start to sniff it like a dog, unable to restrain myself from making a gesture of disapproval, an abstract, tender lick of the tongue. I remember how that after-noon floated above the disarray of glasses and teaspoons, above her box and its crumpled paper. The diorama is as large as one and a half spans of my hand, it has two streetlamps at either end, three awnings painted a rusty red, and three figures. I am one of them, a Sergio Prim within a very large scale: a tiny, cream-colored gentle-man with a hat and cane. To my left, a boy watches the end of the tracks while propping up one of the lampposts with the sole of his shoe and both hands. To my right is a tall lady wearing a tube skirt and gaudy blouse, holding a parasol in her hand. I fear that effigy, Brezo, my friend; I spin as in a dance to avoid looking at her, she looks so lifelike.

I kissed Brezo's hand twice in gratitude. But then I defended myself: "The first and last," I said, touching my image. I didn't mean to seem rude, only to put in practice an old theory regard-ing gifts. Under every gift a hook is hidden, I explained to her, a blunt, caressing hook, but a hook nevertheless—a gaff, a twist on which to catch a web of future compensations. And even when she assured me that she expected nothing in return I felt myself suffocating, overwhelmed. I didn't know how to accept gifts. Of course, I didn't tell her the complete truth. "You've paralyzed me," I should have added. "When I'm with you, I am that man watch-ing a squirrel. I have grown silent, mute. I open your letters with astonishment, for they are extravagant and do not demand replies; your gifts, on the other hand, do. In the end I would knock over the tower of accumulated packages and, annoyed by the racket, the squirrel would run away." All I can do is remain silent, sea swell–Brezo. All I can do is suffer the blows, embrace you, and fall silent. I wish you didn't hear me admitting out loud how in the end the glass had moved without anyone having pushed the table, how Sergio Prim exulted, incredulous at the image of your body in his bed, sang to himself and would have knelt down before you, foolish, foolish, dazzled, dazzled all night long. You must not have been aware of my spirited battle with illusory shapes, with the hallucination that I was watching a program, reaching out my hand, touching your half-naked body, shutting off the unnecessary device of my isolation. These things do not exist, Brezo, they are tricks. These things do not last, the days pass and desire is not kindled. To stand still was to refuse to enter the depths of a forest of infallible boughs. At last, you would grow tired of such a passive man. One morning, the sky clear, visibility high, you would no longer feel the urge to love me—that is where I saw my future sorrow. But at least we would not have stained anything irreplaceable, anything other than sheets and wine glasses. They would catch me, yes, they would catch me, but only after the memory had escaped aboard a plane high above the sea. Though it may seem so, Brezo, my detachment was not motivated by fear. I even fancied myself quite courageous sprawled on the sofa in my house, pushing you away, driving back my protectress, refusing to lower the guard of my own strength. Besides, it is well known that we desire what we do not have. The more I hid, the more you grew. Tell me, was I not courageous? Was I not exceedingly courageous to provoke the full force of your beauty the way I did?

9

On November 1, Brezo launched a sneak attack. Sergio was exhausted after a sleepless night. The waiter in the bar, noticing how tired I was, winked at me: "Mondays. . . . Watch out for Mondays!" God only knows what grand dames he was holding responsible for my evasive, badly shaved face and my dirty shoes. But I let him be. He was right in his own way. I had gotten out of bed in the key of Brezo, and all day Monday resembled a mountain pass she had seized. I offered him a wan smile, partly apologetic, partly complicit. Then a stream of sugar spilled onto my nose, erasing it.

I entered the office crestfallen. My feet left strips of shadow behind on the carpet. The artificial lighting could not conceal the blustery atmosphere, the dense gray sky that had laid siege to us was stationed behind the windows. It is said that the destruction of the Persian hordes that invaded Europe in 480 BC and the retreat of Suleiman the Magnificent from Vienna in 1529 were caused by meteorological phenomena. It is said that Admiral Nelson won his battles with a barometer. I believe it. A city in the rain is cut off from the world; an office in which sheets of water driven by the wind can be seen through picture windows seems otherworldly, as if it weren't located on Calle Príncipe but somewhere in the wilderness. Damp black silk bloomed in the umbrella stands. The office pulsed like a stage after a performance.

It took some work to empty the contents of my folder. A blue envelope leaped from the stream of paper. Candied air, ladies and gentlemen, fruit Brezo was plucking from the passing hours. Yet I hesitated. As if at a concert, silent, trying not to cough, I listened to the music of her correspondence: letters, anachronistic declarations, quotations taken from books, little jokes—the last piece had been a map of the Baltic Sea, shaped like a kneeling man and bearing the following caption: "Sergio Prim implores Brezo not to appear." This time it was an appointment to meet her at six-thirty at the house where she lived with her father.

It had been at least three years since I had last set foot in that place—or the neighborhood for that matter. Brezo lives in one of those neighborhoods that resemble bunkers: there are no stores under arcades or people on the street, the buildings tower like imitations of jutting cliffs, and periodically a blue bus passes next to the parked cars.

I was standing at her doorstep at six-thirty on the dot. I called the elevator and as its doors slid open the doorman emerged like a seer. He must have recognized me as he asked for no explanations, the way doormen always do. Eighth floor, letter D. As Brezo opened the door I remembered how the hallway smelled of shaving cream. At one end stood the same dark closet and as we turned the corner, our bodies inhabited its mirrors for just a moment. As in days gone by, her father, a charming, elderly gentleman with yellow irises, delighted in confounding me with his thoughts on the relationship between quantum mechanics and women. He stood up to shake my hand and invited us to join him in his customary seven o' clock libation. His attire displayed an odd blend of good taste and sloppiness, as if a honed elegance and the clumsiness of an absent man existed side by side.

"My daughter must have told you that I am no longer engaged in research. I am writing a book for laymen on the correspondence between the laws of physics and our feelings of love," he said, stroking his cherry-colored tie. "I firmly believe that a science as young as psychology lacks the theoretical foundations necessary to explain the reactions of the mind. We physicists, given our experience with the laws that govern matter, are best qualified to analyze human behavior. For biographical reasons, I am particularly interested in human behavior with regard to love and am planning on devoting my first volume to this topic."

"Tell him your theory of adultery," Brezo said, spurring him on.

"Adultery, my friend, is my most recent discovery. I have discovered the meaning of infidelity." Don Emilio crossed his legs, revealing a band of flesh that clung to his bone and an elegant sock whose diamonds echoed the color of his tie. "You may have heard of the paradox of Schrödinger's cat," he continued. "That poor animal whose life hangs from a thread that will be triggered by a wave—which would condemn the cat—or by a particle—which would be the cat's salvation. Schrödinger concluded that there was a point at which the cat was neither dead nor alive, for a photon may appear as a particle or a wave, depending on the observer. That is to say, as long as the photon isn't measured, it doesn't exist in either form, just as roses have no color at all when no one is looking at them."

At this point don Emilio sank into a long silence. Later you told me that his reel was turning backward: twenty, thirty, perhaps forty years. A dance. The hair of a bust spun around and around before his yellow eyes. If I were to stop my projector, Brezo, like a lunatic, leave it frozen on the frame of your breasts brushing against me, if I were then to say, come into this cylinder of illuminated air, come and stay with me between the drop of light and the screen, if I were to ask you to do this, if the film never burned when stopped, Brezo, my burning branches, conflagration of my fantasy.

"Then," don Emilio continued, "the lover would be the observer, meaning that only when a woman is with me can I say that she exists, either as a wave or as a particle. Thus all love is adulterous and all adulterous love is Schrödinger's cat, neither dead nor alive as long as we don't possess the woman. When she is not in our arms, my friend, the beloved vanishes. It is pointless to follow or pursue her: no one can be a wave and a particle at the same time. Circular thinking, obsessions, fits of jealousy are all futile. As you can see, quantum mechanics supports a well-known saying: 'Out of sight, out of mind,' or my own version: 'Blind eyes, cold heart.' If men were humble and let themselves be governed by the same principles that govern their atoms they would never again suffer on account of infidelity."

Brezo, who had been attending to our conversation with detached tenderness, stood up before I had a chance to respond.

"We're late," she said, rushing our goodbyes, clutching my arm as she blew her father a silent movie kiss. We walked through the library and the balcony, which had been closed off and turned into a laboratory. Brezo raised the blinds in her room and stood there for a moment, pensively holding the cord. Then she sat down in a mauve rocking chair, banishing me to loneliness of her divan. It was the moment to turn the past into an accomplice, to remember when we had sat right there, talking of Strabo, the geographer-philosopher, to confess that, like a teenager with chewed nails, I was hiding my hands in an attempt to resist the temptation to caress her. It was not to be. Brezo opened fire with no warning at all and placed a dragon with red, forked tongue in the middle of the field: a decision.

"I'm going to a seminar in Santiago next week. Will you come with me?"

A trip. She was proposing we take a trip—I, who have spent just short of half a decade mastering the five hundred square feet of my apartment. Ever since I was a youngster, I've bumped into things. One day someone told me that if mosquitoes were biting me it was because my blood was sweet, and I thought that my clothing must also be sweet, my flesh sweet, and that was why shelves with sharp corners struck my elbows and the edges of sheets of paper amused themselves by cutting imperceptible slits in my fingers and the stairs rose up on tiptoes to throw me down. Years later, Lucía, who would get upset at my clumsiness, concluded that it wasn't that objects were intent on knocking against me but rather, that my leg (for example) would throw itself against the edge of the low table or my ribs would rush to embed themselves in the back of a bus seat. "It's a symptom," she declared, though she immediately switched topics so I never found out what she meant: why I miscalculate the distance that separates my body from the things around it, why I think I am many inches away from the door I am opening when in reality I am so close I am about to slam it against my forehead. In short, I needed six years of Carthusian life in a small bedroom and living room to understand Lucía's system of measurement, the coordinates at which door knockers suddenly threaten to stick themselves up the sleeve of my jacket, the angle at which the glass table is aiming at me. And it occurs to Brezo to propose an odyssey of train cars and luggage, unfamiliar beds and unpredictable breakfasts. Could she have forgotten my reputation for being the only geography student who didn't like to travel? Hundreds of miles and at the end, sandy beaches. What's the point if one always returns home? What's the point if this is where one must contend with time, which never rests? What's the point of taking detours? Brezo-traveler, I am one of those people who decided one day to spend my vacations learning how to stay put.

I flatly refused, and she didn't push me. She came over and sat beside me. Placing one knee on the sofa, she wrapped her long fingers around my face and ignored me when I told her that it wasn't so easy to ask for days off and harder still to change the habits of a prematurely old man. She kissed me slowly on the temples but I refused to yield to her tenderness. To avoid the wounds at the battle's end, Sergio Prim, self-sacrificing prudent knight of advanced age, paladin of politeness, had decided to appear before Brezo as a taciturn mandarin with this motto as the only decoration on his shield: refusal and desire; I don't want gifts, I don't want trips, don't call me but let me kiss you right here and now. I would hide my anguish, feign strength when my position was built on sand, feign mastery.

There is a man who in affairs of the heart, mistrusted behavior obtained through the deployment of premeditated tactics. Yet how are we to understand that after thirty days Brezo had not refrained from bestowing herself, that her passionate gestures remained intact and that she never threatened me with declarations of satisfaction or offense or by suggesting that we spend time together? That woman, who had in the past demonstrated herself to be unyielding, was intent on treating me kindly. On occasion, when we were not alone, I would notice her looking at me, captive of the same childlike flush people display when watching fireworks after the charges have stopped going off and enormous, silent flowers fill the sky. Why did she accompany me with her luminous eyes? She never explained. Why did she never grow weary of my vacillations, why was she not offended whenever my shields jabbed her shoulder, red shields with a white stripe: no entrance, don't look for me, don't need me, don't take another step closer? If I summoned her, she—inexhaustible—would be there at our next date, having forgotten my evasive gestures, her arm trembling at my touch as if I were a prince. So that is what the Three Kings with their three camels represented, heads bowed, arms frozen in the act of offering gold, incense, and myrrh. Was that you? Was that the mystery of adoration?

10

In the days preceding her departure, Brezo couldn't see me because no one could. The office was evaluating areas designated as no-build zones in fifteen outlying municipalities in far too short a time. A young man named Marcos and my friend Enrique were told to report to me. Unaware of the recklessness the agreed-upon deadlines represented, they hounded me with a variety of trivial matters. "Vade retro," my hand in the air would tell them when they came to ask me for instructions. "Vade retro," my white palm told them as it held back the air. Enrique hesitated. Marcos accosted me with minor tasks, poplar trees, birch trees planted in my date book, pine trees on the table, trees that prevented me from seeing the forest. And so the week passed, abounding in ineffectual actions, as it was altogether impossible to complete the study with a shred of integrity in anything less than a month.

When I got home on Thursday, I plunged into the silence, my eyes glazed over, a pathetic specter whose face, bearing a fierce smile and a curly moustache, was first to cross the threshold. The afternoon was dwindling into darkness. Lacking even the momentum to take off my shoes and put on my slippers, to open the junk mail, or to make myself a drink, I collapsed onto the sofa, briefcase still in hand. It was only after a long while that I could summon the strength to turn my head and look at the answering machine. Someone had called. It had to be Brezo, my little red light, Brezo my flashing spark, whispering, here I am, listen to me, listen to me. But Sergio had fallen into a morose silence from which nobody could or should extract him.

Wearily I went looking for an apple. An apple: round and radiant. What a palpable pleasure it was to feel its heft as I leaned against the refrigerator. And you, sir or madam, what do you do? I make apples. Finally a straightforward occupation unencumbered by ethical duplicity, mutilated dreams or nonsense. To make fruit, to engage in the clean activities of agriculture or industry, to join the poorest sectors whose decline professors of structural economics shouted from the rooftops, confident their students would agree. How could we oppose them, we, the vast hordes of future geographers destined for the service section of the pie chart. Ah, the tertiary sector, that amorphous conglomerate of unremittingly useless citizens.

"Sergio! Sergio! Are you there?" Was he dreaming or was she calling him again? But you ought not have come upon me in this state, madwoman, telephoner, my parishioner. You would only frighten yourself with the spectacle of my demagogic life at home. My rage had no object, was inconsolable, so it was only right that it would have no one to converse with. Nobody should set foot on the black grid of my page. Begone, witnesses. I have already been examined once by Lucía, who studied my irascible grimaces, recording every move my inadequate body made. I can't bear witnesses, Brezo, they are the first step toward decrepitude. No one can face life in our stead, and sometimes we are mortified by the sweetness of the others, as if they were making fools of us. The voice stopped immediately. That was when I realized that the apple had been growing, that it was now the size of a watermelon. My jaw could never bite into such a curve, and furthermore I felt anxious and had no appetite. I left the kitchen. Like the boy playing hide-and-go-seek who ducks behind the legs of the adults, I sought refuge in the shifting shadows of a movie, and they sheltered me until sleep arrived.

_11_

The next day Elena Morales's eyes glittered beyond belief, glittered black with tiny flecks of blue when I refused to work on the study any longer. Her voice, in contrast, was filled with an icy calm. While she thought she understood some of my arguments and was willing to find another person to join our team, she invited me to reflect on the propriety of prioritizing the reputation of the office over its performance. "That is to say, if the client prefers a product that is imperfect but ready in short order, it's none of our business," she said, and with calculated deliberation she stood up and walked me to the door.

Sergio alone in the mountains. Dwarfed, disoriented, thirsty, and with no canteen, I found the path and, bewildered, beat my retreat. I hadn't asked for an additional person, but rather, that the entire agency acknowledge that we needed to withdraw from the study. In fact I had walked into the office sure that Elena Morales would ignore my protest even if she pretended to agree with me. But the exact opposite had occurred. The third person came right away. Her name was Nélope, she worked on the sixth floor, sorting data for a two-year-long program carried out in coordination with the Housing Institute, an analysis of how residents divided up space in public housing projects. But she was a professional and had no problem trading two hundred thousand bedrooms for fifteen green zones.

I was hunched over a file cabinet, looking for some folders. I couldn't see well because something was casting a shadow over me. I looked up and there they were. Marcos was nervously running his fingers through his beard; Enrique, a gray-haired king, was absent-mindedly doodling fish in a notebook; Nélope, terribly young, was rocking her uneven black bangs back and forth expectantly. Odd. Very odd. So I was now the veteran journalist, trainer, or sergeant major who rallies his boys before throwing them to the lions. As I listened to them talk about work that needed to be done, it occurred to me that everything was wrong—all of it, from the very beginning, from my initial nervousness at recess when team captains were picking sides, eeny meeny miny moe, while the clumsy ones stood there waiting, our pride evaporated, certain that we would be the last to be chosen. There were three of us, Miguel, Fabián, and I, each in our corner, all of us shamefaced and alone. Today I can almost state as fact that not one of my later disasters—the car accident with my parents, my separation from Lucía—produced such a suffocating knot in my throat as the one that preceded recess when it wasn't raining, when we weren't watching a movie and had nothing to do but form two teams and play cops and robbers, running until we were ready to drop, brushing against the other boys now and then but never managing to grab a single one of them. I failed to catch anyone and suspected with anguish that the secret of life must consist precisely of being able to stop the body that runs through the schoolyard and bumps into us, and I sensed that Miguel, Fabián, and I would always be excluded, just as we were in those dreadful recesses.

But twenty-five years later, when I no longer wanted to grab anyone but wished only for a lizard's hole and a rock, just at that moment, I found myself staring into the eyes of a bunch of athletic, enthusiastic, long-legged youngsters. Team captain at forty—wasn't it a bit late? Wasn't it in fact very late? The fit of grief was gaining ground. I had been trained, however, to be a civilized man: never to make such outbursts in public. I am fascinated by intellect, the way other people play chess in their minds. When I look unruffled I am throwing stones at houses, I am shouting in the wilderness. It's a harmless tactic that sometimes exhausts me, as if it were actually taking place.

Of course the three youngsters had no idea of what was going on. Marcos and Nélope were growing increasingly animated as they talked, while Enrique questioned me gently but persistently. I pressed them to work with all due speed. I didn't say a word about my lack of confidence in the study; quelling one's fears is the tribute that responsibility exacts. They finally left, each one with a mission. I watched as they picked up a phone or pecked at a keyboard with utmost determination.

To close one's eyes, to lean one's neck against the plush wing of an armchair and rest. To unwind. To flee, but not in a whirlwind of miles and hotels or by turning to the ritual of bars and beers to decant my exhaustion into someone else. To flee, but not to my apartment during a period of time when I am particularly vulnerable to obsessions, to the past and its ghosts. To sign a real truce, to wake into an intermission with no commercials or popcorn that could never take place, not in a bar, not in the street, not in the subway. An entr'acte outside the normal course of things. To flee. To rest in a room far from this world.

That incantation reminded me that Brezo was leaving the

next day. Brezo-pursued would be passing through cities hoping to give the slip to something—perhaps someone, perhaps me. I dialed her phone number filled with anxiety. "How are you? What are you going to do?" Her voice was a bolt of lightning: "If it doesn't rain," she announced, "we can go to the park at the Observatory."

12

I still can see you. I suppose there still is a slope in that city that rises to a promontory where a washed-out palace made of gray cement awaits us. Behind it a curved palisade of shrubs and cypress trees still stands where we can peek through the trunks, as if through a battlement. I now know, Brezo, that surrender and cowardice were both out of the question. I need to speak to you about remembering one's dreams, about a nostalgia, green as algae, about a disembodied dome poised over the trees, and this is real, is part of life as well, though others might take you up in planes or show you events that leave you pale, never-ending conversations, vaults of stone.

I waited for you in the park at the Observatory. I first caught sight of you at the foot of the hill, your chestnut-brown hair and an enormous black overcoat that rendered your whole body shapeless. You were running up the hill, concerned perhaps that you were late. You waved at me. I am, my friend, a creature of emotion. Come hither, I said to you silently. But what will we do with reality afterward? What will we do with her movie actress hairdo, her evening dress, her red parasol? I know her, Brezo. I know how the dark blue of her irises shines like the sweaty rumps of horses, that the gleaming on her left wrist is not a watch but a simple pearl bracelet. She has been prowling my street the last few days, and I should warn you that she is watching us. Be afraid, my friend, of that figure. She employs her elegance so that we will forget that she resembles a police inspector. When the presumed innocent knocks on the door, the inspector is stroking the evidence of the crime that sits on his desk while he feigns pleasantries, takes pleasure in giving false hope to the criminal. The proof she holds as she waits for us is passion, its mortality, its tendency toward disorder. And her reason for lying in wait like this is a night spent in my apartment. There were two naked bodies, and I swore I wouldn't slip up, dissect the stag, domesticate the bird.

Reality already had us surrounded when the wind ruffled your profile, interrupting it with branches or strands of hair. You leaned against the trunk of a cypress tree, soon afterward a whirlwind spun into life and I was blinded by several grains of sand. I walked over to you, rubbing my eyes. Your hand reached through the air, attempting to take mine. Adding to the irritation of my scratched eyes was my anxiety born of the growing esteem in which you held me. It tends to happen to me after an expression of affection or when people I admire declare their confidence in me: I am filled with unease, an inability to stay put; in short, a need to vanish into thin air to avoid having to face the gift. I am like those modern vases that barely stand up; we only have to pour in a little too much water or put in too big a bouquet and they are vanquished: the water spills out and they break apart. I have neither the capacity nor the solidity to hold you, Brezo. That was what I wanted to tell you, but I was inspired by your vaguely melodic murmuring:

"Do you know," I asked, "Claude Debussy's claim that 'music does not lie in the notes but between the notes'?"

She did know it, ladies and gentlemen. Her singing teacher

used to quote it to tell her students how to breathe. Brezo, Brezo, instrument of mine, do you refuse even this explanation?

"It is my opinion," I continued, "that while some men strive for the dense, colorful glory of painting, others harness all their yearnings to achieve the invisibility of music: to be not in things but between them."

Languorously—as if in reclaiming a sleeping memory you had grown sleepy yourself—you recalled the eve of your fourteenth birthday. It is early, the floor of your house is quite cold. An adolescent Brezo, wearing a nightgown and slippers, knocks on the door of don Emilio's office. Standing on tiptoes, leaning against the radiator, you tell him that for your birthday you want a space bar. "I don't understand," don Emilio says. "You are a scientist," responds the rhetorical impertinence of your youth. "Invent a space bar, like the one on typewriters but bigger: one that works for life, so that if I pressed it in the movie theater, for example, empty seats would appear between my seat and the one next to me." Don Emilio, I imagine, contained his impatience and sent you back to bed.

"We never talked about that again," you said, your voice growing hard. "My mother had run off with the Irishman. I had other things on my mind."

Within a few months your mother had died of leukemia. When you told me this I took it for granted that this was your hobbyhorse. But two crosspieces are needed to form a cross, and one was missing: the totality of fragments that threw your life story out of kilter, a perpendicular piece I would have a hard time finding, for I had begun to love you, crazy one, and love—despite all claims to the contrary—is the offering of tributes to ignorance.

"You see, you aren't alone. We all have fantasies of making our escape," you concluded. "But at your age?"

What, I thought, is my age? At what age exactly do adults leave their ill-defined and inappropriate spirit behind? Did I miss this moment, did I forget to change trains? But all I could do was smile, ridiculous woman. A space bar, you say.

"Haven't you ever wished again," I asked, "at a party, on a job, after making a mistake, to press your bar and have an empty space appear?"

The map of the city we will always inhabit, the necessary combination of smooth knees and dull shoulders that marks the bodies we desire, these are decided in our imagination without our realizing it. That is why, Brezo, you were about to say the name of my dwelling.

"A hollow," you said under the Observatory arcade.

A hollow, Brezo, a hollow. Most people are set upon a single place, orchards, windmills, or palaces, and want to flee there. All well and good. But how do they plan to protect those places? And how can a sanctuary offer them happiness when they need to protect it?

I nodded timidly, a failed gesture as your eyes were contemplating a private, inner filmography. Meanwhile it had begun to rain. I cautiously let drop a suggestion: "Shall we go . . . ?" I could have dropped a china cup the way you rushed—why, oh why?—to catch it.

The rain kept falling for the rest of the afternoon. A haze of drowsiness produced by the drumming water precedes us into the house, ladies and gentlemen. My sadness resembles the upper part of a lip bitten by its nervous owner. But I had Brezo with me, I tousled the thousand expressions of her face, oh, her face: that hoisted, muddy sail, that small, white canvas shaking in the wind, my body stretched out like the deck of a boat.

13

Against physiology. Against the human need to be hugged, touched, delicately licked by an expert tongue. I want to write against physiology because physiology is impossible. I don't want to leave my sanctuary and enter life, I don't want to go out to the stores to buy canned food or rice; you are my shell, Brezo, I want to stay inside you. But a man must go out when the night sinks into the dumpster and sixty-cylinder monsters roar by their side. I will remain steadfast in my resistance to physiology, will never undress, will stand like a Japanese painter. Never naked, never trusting that I might ever abandon my responsibility again, as when the rain tapped on the windowsills, when you were my room and my memory.

The wind passed its hand over the drenched crowns of the trees, drops laughing as they fell. As the first streetlamps were coming on, a sudden brightness shone in the window; you stretched out my body with your slender arms and every one of your sighs was like a step downward, a descent from the cross, a descent from the mirrors, laughter in a pit like an abyss that opened onto Australia, its great plains and sky of red suns.

"Why?" Your voice, just emerging from the swoon you had fallen into, was trying to find me.

"What do you mean, why?"

"Why is it so easy?" you said, and sank back into your languor, stretched out to my left, your eyes closing.

Soon it will stop being easy, Brezo. You are the emphasis I never had, you are the alacrity placed in front of my monotony. I am an introverted man, an underground spring, a trapped current, while you, waterfall, are an extrovert who paints pieces of the atmosphere soaking white. You do not know the word reserved or how to store away images and emotions for the winter. And if you are the cicada, thrumming in a perpetual summer, how could you understand the danger lurking in our lack of provisions, how can I explain to you that Prim is a skinny book, that one quickly reaches the last page and there is nothing left but wretched desolation?

I felt in my shoulder that Brezo was looking around for the time. "I still have to pack my bags," said the feline lamp lighting my bedroom. She got up without a sound. The black and white stripes of the shower curtain unfurled from left to right—a series of photograms. The falling water was a clapboard signaling reality's entrance.

14

Having decided to speak, I must tell all. There is no such thing as an innocent sentiment. I had dreamed up Brezo, and for that I was to blame. I'm lying: I belonged to Brezo. With bitten lips I got her into my bed, and she was the one biting them, feverish with happiness. Sergio had begun to court her without any hope. At inopportune moments, on inopportune days, she would seek my friendship. She gave me a full report on her lovers, made me an accomplice in her craziness, needed—I imagine—to see herself reflected in someone else, to check her image through the distortions of my composed and elusive mistrust. But Brezo, flanked by men who were not at all short, never spoke to my body. Her shoulders didn't press forward, calling to me, she didn't extend her lips toward mine. After we completed our degrees, I embarked on forgetfulness while she embarked on her journey to the North. Lucía appeared on my first job. She would open her eyes wide when she spoke on the phone. I would watch her take off on a red Vespa, her cheek pressed against the back of a boy with a beard. For that brief period in my life, Brezo faded away. I pursued Lucía relentlessly. At my belated age I would accompany her to exclusive bars where the frenetic bodies of curvaceous dancers glistened under the lights. I would watch her dance.

There are woman who shine and women who are black holes. Lucía was a black hole with the beauty of a black hole. When her eyes turned inward, forming a distant vector with her dark hair, that was when I loved her the most. When Lucía was a black stone, a black and inaccessible shadow, far away, that was when I loved her the most. I lived with her, always fearful of misplacing her. I got engaged to marry her the way someone watches over something with such care that the day he finally goes to get it, he has no idea where it is.

But there are women who shine. They are more fragile, they are women whose features sometimes go unnoticed until, without warning, they shine: a green light in the hair, the glistening of moist eyes, a lamp's radiance beneath the lips all sparkle together, producing a tenuous, permeable portrait. In the days leading up to my separation, resplendent Brezo became a condition. On many occasions, taking advantage of the anonymity provided by a group of friends, I would split in two. I would order rum—because that's what she drank—and would let myself be carried away by the rhythm of an invisible oscillation. I would pretend to pay attention to the gathering of common memories, humorous remarks, retorts and rejoinders, turbulent games. But a woeful voice had given the order: dive, dive. And so I dove. I watched them all through the affability of alcohol, my occasional remarks were genial, even witty. Meanwhile my body was moving to another plane. One day at dawn I happened to be sitting at the end of a booth seat and could clearly see my double torso leaning out like a roly-poly toy. Then I watched myself leave. Dark rum, my head in a daze, and I with Brezo. Brezo: territory of my solitude.

If a man slips away to dream while in the company of others, what won't he do when he is by himself? The ocean blended with the sky on the walls of my bedroom, the day moved across the horizon of an indistinct baseboard, and who would have dared to compete with my fertile, imaginary gardens when the key no longer clicked in the lock and no one—no one—came to soothe my inner torment, though no one was about to interrupt my beatific trances either. Reverie entered peacefully, stripped bare of words, the metronomic heart of music, and a bright and cloudy light spun over the crowns of the trees.

Then Prim closed himself up. A very long X made of Scotch tape would cover him whenever he took public transportation, went to work, or bought socks. An invisible X, Brezo, the crossed stripes of an absent man. You were far away; I was your stolen mailbox full of letters I had written in my head but never put down on paper. I would leave my house, cross the street, and would already be telling you of my little adventures, your eyes of tea shining before me. Gradually I learned to dilute you, my desire probed lifeless hallways and perched on doors. And now you are completing yourself. Listen to me, Brezo: a man cannot stretch any farther. In my mind I fancy myself walking with you to the top of mountains, I grow tired, but the snow gets in our shoes, the summit is filled with cars, for sometimes the mountains cannot stretch any farther either, but are merely tourist attractions. Brezo, oh Brezo, I had no idea that dreams are not perpetrated with impunity. Whom can I ask for mercy?

15

The next day, while I was paying for my jars of vegetables, my fish and my cheese at the supermarket, Brezo was hoisting her bag into the overhead compartment of a train heading for Zamora, where she would make the first of her many stopovers. They were days filled with vertigo. She would call and I would ask, as if disoriented, where are you? Strange towns, strange people provided Brezo a room in their house, and this was the way she charted her route to the Atlantic. "I don't want to rest, I want to exhaust myself," she would say about her meanderings. This reminded me of the morning she applied for the fellowship in Finland. We were returning from the Ministry, she was silent like a sulky child until it occurred to her that what she needed to do was to eat some backpacks. Brezo loved rituals, and now I wonder if it was by communing with blue and red scraps of nylon that she reclaimed the impulsiveness of her teenage years.

Once she got to the seminar, at least she was always calling from the same city though she continued to choose phone booths in indeterminate locations, with religious music, howling, or a youthful racket in the background. She would usually call around ten at night and I would let the phone ring two or three times before answering in an attempt to inject myself with common sense. I would talk to her standing up, holding the base of the phone in one hand and the receiver in the other, taking care not to let the slightest trace of anxiety reach Brezo, that is, toning down as best I could the mournful inflections people use who have not spoken to anyone in over four hours, averting any reference to my problems at work, my lack of motivation, my feeling of unease at not being able to hide myself in her body as I would in a pile of dry leaves. To make her laugh was practically my sole objective. To provoke her laughter, make it grow, and keep it going, my mind would work at a feverish pace. Later, after I hung up, I would seem to hear a sound like that of ice cubes knocking against one another in glasses. They were the waves of her laughter that I would revisit, sprawled on the sofa.

Her last call was different. Three hours before her train was going to leave, a woman of indeterminate age could be seen striding around Santiago gathering coins, a sort of mime dressed in black with nearly transparent eyes in search of a public telephone that was not in use. Brezo's voice rang in my house with some anticipation. It arrived as if filtered through the grille of an old confessional rather than a telecommunications network. Apparently she had met a friend in a bar with whom, several years ago, she had had an upsetting relationship. "You know, I have old flames like lingering colds," she said, and got lost in an unrelated story from her emotional life. I listened silently to the cast of characters who at one time or another had populated Brezo's gaze, her waist. "They return," she said. "They always return—as memories, as letters, as dreams, they come looking for me, show up in cafés, at the end of movies. You appeared to me at a bus stop." Sergio, caught off guard, ate those words like a piece of cookie in Alice's woods: growing smaller and smaller, Sergio Prim now took up the minute space of a period, the final bastion from which no one could throw him out. Far away, on a dark and almost empty street, Brezo continued talking to me in zigzags. Her stories made me think of the tops of trees swaying, full and tremulous in the rivers. I listened to them without losing my composure for I had realized that it was my retiring nature Brezo was seeking, nothing less than my rock-solid spot, however small it might be. Holding to my strict vocation of solitude, I played the role of a leaning post, a column, or the simple trunk of a traffic light so you would have something to lean on. You, expelled and contained woman, point-less woman, you and your comings and goings, your old flames like lingering colds, your outlandish faith in an indestructible and imaginary—imaginary, my friend—Sergio Prim.

The bedroom goes into hiding, the walls, the bed, the windows duck down as I draw the memory, and I no longer know if what I had embarked upon was sufficient cause of my madness or whether it is truly of no use to anyone, whether any of you readers ever wished to cleave the surface of the world for your potential beloved, for the nightmare that is erased. Perhaps none of you ever wished to stand behind your beloved, holding up a hollow like a coat, a moment of peace, its sleeves floating in the air, to help her put it on and then to say, come here and rest.

16

Even faster than the train bringing Brezo back were the circumstances that arrived and embraced me in a circle of stress and irascibility. Whether I was seeking relief from the compromises I'd made with Elena Morales or was moved by the stag-like fear triggered by certain classic expressions of affection, instead of going to pick Brezo up at the station, I accepted Enrique's offer. Hidden, concealed by the white saddle of his eyebrows, Enrique had noticed my attempt to contain gestures that were emerging nonetheless: blowing air through my lips like a camel or drumming pens on the table. Without consulting me, the way one might treat someone who is experiencing a momentary fit, he led me to an Indian restaurant, ordered food, then dragged me from one glass of wine to another through a blur of bars at four, six, seven in the evening. I let him do it, Brezo. I was delaying the moment when I would have to come face-to-face with your return, like someone who stops short at a hastily drawn sketch for fear of pursuing the drawing more seriously.

Cats, urban development, the proportions of a woman: Sergio followed the conversation as through a haze. Now and then a particular term would come into focus—the name "Bailén" attached to a post—and he would let his spirit linger in that street, and with no one else around, blasts of loneliness, feline and incongruous, would emanate from his eyes; so you hadn't waited for her. Enrique was watching me, apparently he had asked me a question. He wanted to know if I had a girlfriend. I slowly opened my lips. "No," I said, partly out of shock and partly out of sadness. I will betray you again and again, Brezo. They will say your name to me and I will deny you, will not know you, will display a look of surprise so that no one will know I know you. The words of an old activist, a clandestine lover; the fear of naming, of saying "This is a tree" or perhaps "She has come," "She will go." I will hold my silence. To protect you from that woman with the dress cut low in the back I must convince her that I never knew you, that you never existed, that it was all an illusion born of spite.

Night fell and we lay slouched in the large armchairs of a bar filled with prints of gymnasts from the late nineteenth century. A young woman walked by—was it you? No, it wasn't—she headed for the coat room and then we watched as she came out wrapped in a faded green cloak. The clock on the wall struck seven scathing strokes. How many flashes was that? Perhaps fifteen hundred: the tiny red bulb flashing seven hundred and fifty times off and seven hundred and fifty times on just so that, when I opened my front door I would know that you had called. Every minute I spent in that bar turned into additional flashes, your exhausted brightness beating and unbeating: Please, Enrique, let's go.

At the bus stop I found myself surrounded by women who had reinvented their lips: roses shaped like "o"s, red as decals. A number 37 opened its doors; escorted by the cluster of passengers, Brezo did not get off. I got on the bus with the slowness of a man lost in thought; the men pushed me, the women rubbed their children's heads against me. On the other side of the glass, a river of impatient car horns. Let there be silence, let emptiness fill the luminous capital. I want my eyes to float over Brezo's body. And yet, what is a body? In my case, identity squeezed between a depleted head of hair and a dull pair of shoes. Perhaps that is why I have to work so hard to hold my body up, so hard that I have to use other muscles support myself, other feet and other shoulders to escape it, the way one leaves a bicycle leaning against a wall.

17

Certain minerals—slate, mica—possess a foliaceous structure, but so do certain psychologies, that is to say, human psychology in general is constructed so it tends to turn into thin sheets. One swift hit and the self shatters, one slight mishap and the sheets come crashing down, and as they fall, whatever surface they meet smashes them to bits. My series of fractures, my fragile day began with an accident a home. I got soap in my left eye which stung and turned red. My spirit suddenly split in two, as if half of Sergio were sad or had caught a cold or was suffering from a spring allergy.

At the office the cobalt blue sky crowded the only window left uncovered. Below it was a new table with its computer and Nélope, who did not turn to greet me. I was sorry not to see Enrique's smile of complicity, a veiled allusion to the previous afternoon. He needed to speak with me, she said. I took off my overcoat and went looking for him. He showed me a memo establishing a work schedule different from the one I had proposed for our study. Taken aback, my first sheet smashed to bits, I called Elena Morales. No answer.

They no longer trusted me. Doña Elena must have considered my complaints about us not having enough time absurd. Not knowing what to do, I slipped into my oldest document, "Assessments of Landscape I." My god, there was once a time when I believed in my work. The landscape seen as a resource. That tunnel of shadows the alder trees form over the river. . . . Prim was fifteen years old, the rest of the campers have packed up the tents, are leaving, but he has forgotten something—perhaps his red Swiss army knife with seven tools. He rushes back, we watch him crouch down and—how strange: he isn't feeling around on the ground the way someone would who is searching for something. Prim just stands there, committing things to memory: a flat, rocky terrace, the shaded edge of the water, the roots of trees, the peaceful blend of colors that no longer disturbs the sleeping bags left to air out on the tents, those rows of brilliant smudges, not even that shred of green felt from a canteen floating in the water. It's been many years now since I began to collect redemptive images and then project them onto the yellow and black columns in the garage, my desktop at school, a screen between me and my cousins' mean faces.

For the first few months after I started working in doña Elena's office, I thought I had found the job of a lifetime: I was a landscape detector. In those days I carried out the semi-administrative duties of a contract employee in the Ministry of Transportation, and I assure you that mine was a fortunate fate for someone who did not want to teach. The country, meanwhile, was moving forward. New regulations required that projects to build large industrial plants, public works, or urban initiatives be accompanied by impact statements, that is, a study of the repercussions the project would have on the hydrology, the economy, the climate—that is to say, the landscape. What more could a geographer want? Elena Morales, a petite and intelligent professor, had left her department to start one of the first agencies dedicated to this type of work.

And she wrote to me, offering me a job. Her invitation was not, she emphasized, based solely on academic criteria but also on the impact of a memory. It had been during a seminar on the post-industrial city she'd offered on her return from a conference in Peru. My classmates had gotten interested in the country and she started to talk about standards of living and economic problems until she reached the Andean region. It seems that with persistent and pointed questions I had attempted to figure out what it was about these questions that interested her. This was why she had thought of me for a job that consisted precisely of formulating and solving these types of questions.

I save that letter like the ace of hearts with which I won the first hand, though the circular stain of a glass on the sideboard and a lingering smell of gin are all that remain of the loot I acquired. Nevertheless, during those first few months I knew victory. It was as if that boy Sergio Prim had been given a private watchtower over that river of alder trees and asked, "Where can we set up our tents so they aren't visible, or should we just prohibit any camping within a five-mile radius?" I studied everything I could lay my hands on relating to landscapes, from the ancient Greeks to present times. I had articles translated from Bulgarian and Danish, I read the masters of the Renaissance and attempted to reconcile their maxims—*viz.*, "Water in motion is always beautiful"—with modern concepts of the watershed, of fragility or susceptibility to deterioration. But right away—take note, Brezo—*right away* reality showed up, clicking her heels, frivolous, and slowly chewing an idiotic phrase: fraudulent schemes. Sweetened schemes, friendly, strawberry-filled, "everyday" schemes, oblique schemes that materialized just as I was collecting data and that prevented me from being fair. On the whole, what we were producing, my friend, were letters of marque, licenses to do whatever one wishes. "The minority is our vindication," doña Elena whispered to me one night several years ago. We were the last ones to leave the office, and when we realized we were both heading for the same pub, we began to confide in one another. Since then, when we spoke of our convictions, we made no mention of that initial conversation: it had been draped in the thick, white sheet of oblivion. In contrast, differences in methodology frequently resulted in needless friction between us, raspings of the soul, chafing that knew nothing of your breasts against mine, impalpable Brezo, distant Brezo.

Sometimes nothing happens—the heart is distracted—and sometimes everything happens at once. Marcos came in search of bibliographies, the phone rang, I was just about to delete a file by mistake. Within minutes I was excessively agitated, was making incomplete and pointless gestures over and over, was blinded by error messages on the computer screen. The telephone rang once more. I waited for it to stop, and then fled from that cacophonous room, that raucous hub of urban planning.

Wind swept the street. The pigeons in the Plaza Santa Ana parted as I came near. I entered a telephone booth and this time, this time it was I who called Brezo:

"Welcome, traveler. I got your message but there was trouble at work, and I don't know if I can see you."

"Anything serious?"

"Not really."

"Are you down in the dumps?"

"I guess so." Acknowledging this flew in the face of my theories, but her voice lulled me into submission and sometimes the temptation to give the king a little push is irresistible: one less round to play, the toppled, rolling piece, the blameless piece now lying on the board.

Imagine, readers, a man sporting his first gray hairs, a short man with a large head, a man alone and full of sorrow in his gray suit in a telephone booth surrounded by pigeons. Perhaps you are familiar with the desolation of the Plaza Santa Ana during a week when it is cold and windy, a newspaper crashing into the legs of benches, the broken amber of bottles scraping the ground, and not a soul in sight. At that altar of propped-up houses, before a congregation of madwomen and sleeping drunkards, I invoked your image. Your ten days of absence rose like roller coasters from whose summit I hurled myself:

"Pay no attention to me. Can you come to my house today . . . at five?"

Walking back to the office, my hands were crossed at my back, my bearing contrite, but my face was full of delight. I imagined meeting you in less than three hours. I saw us embracing in my bedroom and in the background were several figures the size of clover: my colleagues, our clients, an Elena Morales in a short, white cloak, and a fearful and mutinous Sergio Prim.

No sooner had I opened the door than Enrique asked me for data I didn't have. Was I wrong to refuse to gather them with such haste and imprecision? Did this reflect my integrity or perhaps my incompetence? How do we stamp our actions with confidence? Everyone in the office seemed to have mastered this skill as the agency grew ever larger until it dominated the foreground of my imagination, relegating you and me to the farthest reaches of the background, transformed into stones, threads, tiny figures in Bosch's maelstrom. I answered Enrique with a mixture of agitation and timidity entirely befitting a superior. Suddenly I found myself uninterested in my own arguments. In my distraction, I considered walking with him over to a far corner by the column and speaking frankly to him. Enrique, I would say, how do you manage to stay calm? What does Marcos do to always look contented? But I kept quiet and went to get a café au lait. Leaning against the wall, dressed in a sienna-colored suit that looked like a toga, Elena Morales was talking—arguing, it seemed—with the agency's lawyer, Juan Peña.

I pressed the button that said "BLACK"—I always take my coffee with sugar, but sometimes the roundness of a word can save us, its bulbous *B* becomes the depository of our bile, its *A* wards off the abysses into which we might have fallen.

"I didn't see you there, Mr. Prim," doña Elena said when the machine beeped, telling me to take my beverage. "I owe you an explanation."

In a heartfelt and concerned tone of voice she apologized for not having let me know earlier. Apparently I was going to be entrusted with a confidential impact statement. Doña Elena hadn't wanted to write to me about it on the computer for fear that another employee might see the message. She decided to tell me first thing in the morning but hadn't had a minute free. She asked me to come to her office the next day, just stop by. The coattails of the lawyer's jacket were swaying by her side. I smiled, accepted her explanation, and left right away. My concerns of the last few days were drained of all meaning but didn't vanish. Rather, like a sealed-up window, like a condemned dresser, they absurdly invaded my inner chambers. Curves, not of a woman but of unraveled wool, curves of an accordion described my spirit.

Oh, undaunted one, unscathed one, my shifting desire is the surface of an agitated liquid by your side. I was wavering, Brezo. I was sinking without that upsetting misunderstanding with doña Elena to justify my affliction. Sadness, my friend, rarely proceeds from the outside; it is local. I lament the errors I have committed.

In the end we are the ones who bring sorrow upon ourselves, we are the object of our nostalgia, of the rain. Sadness is always redundant. And with each footstep, Prim could more clearly distinguish the label that named his destiny: one of many tables, not to be first in his class, a weariness in his chest and the fear that Brezo could tell.

18

When I opened the door, time condensed in a centripetal embrace; the insides of your arms circling my back like an orbit. There was no hesitation, like the stone dropped from the Tower of Pisa, the apple Newton observed, the wheel stopped by inertia. My hands settled on your breasts like a head on a headrest, the way the lid on a tea kettle turns until it can turn no more.

Blue and gray squares dominated the surface of my bedspread and above them, you, arching your body, your back filled with light. You were spinning, throwing off sparks and saying "Take me." The command leaped from your mouth in a smooth mixture of lust and candor. I joined you in the driver's seat of fleeting pleasure. The room filled with sketches of you. There were, say, ninety Brezos for every minute I remember. I loved them all, never tiring, for lovers are blind as bats and fated to act as if they have no idea what's going on, as if no one had told them the sky isn't blue and they don't realize that the joining of mammals is the weakest joint of all. A split orange, an egg cracked in half, a pair of cherries pulled apart. No resemblance even to two hands clasping or the fork of two branches: we are sections of fruit that have been pulled apart, skinny sections cast adrift, ephemeral passion and trembling legs.

But desire refuses us, desire robs our sanity and I was so close to my dream, fully prostrate there, altogether destroyed by it when I led you with my flesh. Where were we heading, Brezo?

Something overflowed, a gust of wind hit the window or maybe it was you. You had accidentally knocked over a glass, broken our unspoken pact that all was provisional. You were trying, for the first time, to nail down the future.

"You should come to Finland," you said.

Though this was not an actual proposal, I was frightened. Danger, that triangle of slippery surfaces. What a sign to post! When you summon me, you dodge the traps, rupture the agreement that you shall not place your feet on the ground, that you shall inhabit the seconds like ghost ships that will forever refrain from attacking.

You turned, light reflected off the marble laid under the cheeks by consummated pleasure. We started to get dressed. My friend, are explanations of any use? "Forget the invitation," I would have asked you. "Don't you realize that resistance leads to offense and acceptance to catastrophe?" No, you didn't understand. Reckless, you were about to send me a messenger, a hopeful "What do you think?," a page standing out in the cold. I didn't say a word. In my family, Brezo, they always said the cat had gotten my tongue. Between my cousins, aunts, and grandmothers, I had been defined and accused. Until one day I decided to prove them right. If Sergio had no tongue then they wouldn't hear another word from me. You didn't know about this—how could you have? A man reaches a certain age, wounds and all, and it is best that he be left alone so no one touches him by accident. I call the architects from my cloistered bedroom, Brezo, send out floor plans, materials. I want to construct a propitious place for you, but not by your side. I know that by your side I would make mistakes. I gestured to the page, who was still standing there waiting, and this is what I said: "Inform your mistress that Prim is a skeptic." You opened the window and in came the cold air and the sound of the rain that had started to fall again. I tried to explain myself but my mind grew soft like that of a drunk, a drunk sponge cake, and what could I possibly say? Ladies and gentlemen, this individual was operating on blind stubbornness, is afflicted by a kind of fear, a panic of all things convex, of the spiky ridges of the day, of reality that puffs up and hurls us off the precipice?

We had passed from twilight into darkness. Through my bedroom window a luminous mist, an omen, grew thicker. Two derricks offered their blessings in the distance. It was the hour when the weariness of the day is revealed, when it pours from every corner of the house and we wish to be by ourselves.

You discreetly gave my shoulder a sudden squeeze, then looked for your wristwatch, your hairclips, your multicolored scarf. "It's late," you said. I thought of those traveling salesmen who spread myriad objects around the room and then gather them up in the blink of an eye. That is how you gathered yourself up, my little automatic umbrella: you not only opened by yourself, you closed as well. Wandering Brezo, night fell and you left the building, expelled by my unsociability.

I spied on you through the window, watched you stride from one sudden bus stop to the next, crossing the street, as you are wont to do, without looking either way. Your clothes had not yet harmonized with your body, so it was easy to imagine your shoulder blades gently pushing against your blouse. With your back to me, you waved goodbye as you turned the corner. Your hand, one more letter without a return address: I'm not writing so you will write back, I am not sending you greetings to get a response, it seemed to say. Standing at the window, Sergio waved a handkerchief you didn't see, scratched with quivering fingers at the envelopes lacking return addresses that would allow me to respond. Brezo, life comes and happens to us far away, like snow falling in a glass ball it happens to the people we never were. While you spoke quiet words to me, Sergio stalked your waist, impulsive and meek with gratitude.

19

Elena Morales's new assignment lent itself to my goal of drawing the outline of an open space. The "confidential" impact statement consisted of the analysis of the environmental, social, and economic ramifications of a military heliport in the Cuenca valley, high in the mountains. Hunched over an unattended keyboard, sheltered by countless charts and thick reports, I pushed forward in search of the spot. Oh, ladies and gentlemen, dear readers, introverted minds, tell me whether, the way a length of silk that falls over a sleeping body temporarily adopts its shape, Brezo will want to stretch out over the conquests of my vocabulary. Come:

Imagine that you are looking at the hollow of your hand. Now imagine that you take your hand away, leaving the hollow—as if we had removed the tree from a hollow tree, as if we had removed the wall from a hollow wall or the wooden panels and rod with all its hangers and hanging clothes from a closet. Consider the precise dimensions of the word hollow. Pay no attention to the container, no matter how empty it might be. Every container is a source of danger: a caterpillar might emerge from the bloody pit of an apricot; the homeowner from a spacious house, a spider web lurks like an enemy in the back of the foyer. I was trying, Brezo, to find you that place unencumbered by worry and marked by an intimate and benign invisibility.

One Saturday I finally decided to call her. She was going to introduce me to some friends of hers, a tricky operation, an unfortunate situation. The bar swallowed Brezo whole, blouses and heads of flowing hair swirled around her like smoke. For the first hour I tried to follow her down black passageways. I returned to the bar worn out, and she would come looking for me now and then. At one point she took me to meet the blond devourer of archives who was standing with a velvet girl. Then five or six other acquaintances appeared and they all drank and spoke compulsively. All except for the velvet girl. Meticulously groomed, two or three shocks of hair falling over her eyes, the fragile girl watched her companions. She wore a garnet-colored tailored suit bearing six unnecessary buttons that accentuated her bosom which she covered with one hand while displaying the excessive attentiveness of those who are uncomfortable in crowds. I imagined her to be a reader, a voracious reader— books, Brezo, as you are learning, were our courage: attending the parties in the Saint Germain *faubourg* without being seen, admiring the butterfly-like dress of the Duchess of Guermantes, courting, seducing, without worrying about appearances. The velvet girl, a version of me, left. It was getting late. I was tired but pushed on, noticing a slight aftertaste of rum on my tongue. Then I noticed Brezo's hand resting on my back and the perfume on her neck assaulted me. I wanted to wring her dry, climb shamelessly down her cleavage, drunk, utmost, but Sergio was intent on talking to her, and requested an audience.

We went to the cafeteria in a hotel with a Nordic name. With her blaze of hair and circles under her eyes, delicately covered by sunglasses, she looked like a foreigner in southern climes.

"Why do we stare at one spot and not at another?" I asked and took her hand. "Whenever we feel harassed or in the dark or depressed, why do we choose to rest our eyes on this wall socket or that glazed tile?"

She looked a bit puzzled.

"Brezo, could you just stare at the light reflected in a glass and know its meaning? Could you lose yourself like those monks that speak of non-being while at the same time—and this is the difference with the monks—staying present with me?"

I remember a bustling of customers, young ostriches with short skirts, mature men with backs like dark blue slabs of stone. Brezo thought I was drunk and indeed I was, drunk enough to set conditions for her, my apparition, drunk enough to show her those spots—hollows—those regions of emotion that offer us shelter. We should stop seeing each other.

That was when you took off your sunglasses.

"I don't believe you," you said, and you were right. You were right to doubt: life is dubious, it is reasonable not to believe anything. Brezo, if only you could not believe in the cars parked by the door, not believe in those highball glasses, not believe in me. That woman with the long gloves and mane of straight hair, that woman we are looking at is a lie and her long-legged gait was invented by the movies. Don't believe anything, my friend, not the white walls nor the tender trombones nor the factories that light up in the night. Don't believe the voice that seems to chime from the clocks nor the smell of coffee nor the silence—not even the silence. Don't believe the images of unfettered pleasure that come to perch on your languor, don't believe your languor. And when people tell you how they are feeling, don't believe a word of it, however difficult that might be. Look at me, so far away, with willows outside the window. My friend, I now doubt the willows, the window, the radiator, the cold. In this era of light switches, when I cannot tell whether the phonograph needle is touching the record, because a bolt of lightning is touching it, who will assure me that, by flicking a switch, I didn't accidentally turn on a light bulb in France, that I was careful enough not to leave the streetlamps on a street in Córdoba without electricity, that no one turned me on? You should know that you would supply me with electricity right now if you touched me, if you just brushed your knees against mine. . . . But you don't have to believe me. Don't ever believe this haphazard jargon of mighty love, Brezo. Don't give any credence to the scrap of paper they bring us with numbers written on it, nor to my nose, nor to my legs as they walk forward. Where are they headed? "Don't believe anything," I said, leaving the money for our drinks on the table. And when our bodies finally collapsed on top of each other, bathing in each other's energy, I said once more: don't believe anything because, at the least, you will be protecting a sensitive, almost liquid, shifting, and turbulent system that is somewhat mysteriously called your sense of humor.

20

Work again took on a diffuse hostility. Elena Morales's venerable face, her deliberate manner made me just as uncomfortable as did my colleagues' efficiency. With the excuse that the fluorescent lights were hurting my eyes, I adjusted my table so it sat between the column and the wall. This new arrangement reinforced my isolation. When people wanted to pass behind me, they had to slip sideways by the column, nudge my chair, and then skirt the corner of the table by an inch or two. But even these measures didn't help me maintain a certain level of coherence in my halting research. Every other second the telephone would ring, and the people prowling around my workspace put me on edge because I didn't want anyone to catch sight of my smuggled books. Until the day when, in one of these books, I came across the description of a suitable location. The author, Bernardo Soares, referred to a visit he made to his office at an unusual time of day, commenting, "It was, after a fashion, home—that is to say, the place one doesn't feel at." Soon after reading this, Sergio announced that he wished to stay in the office after everyone had left, to avoid the needless exposure, so he said, of military data.

By six that evening the office would empty, and the cleaning ladies would arrive at eight. So I had two hours to look for documentation, any reference at all, a single word like a cry of encouragement. As soon as I heard the last employee leave I pulled out my materials from the filing cabinet: index cards I'd filled during the weekend at the library, readings, old notes from my university days. I found myself particularly drawn to the geographers of perception, a tendency that has scarcely merited an epigraph in the syllabus, but whose contributions to the field include the "mental map." Oh, delicious idea. Oh, tripartite formulation of the world. Neither inside nor outside exists, no man stands inside his house while the surface of avenues and boulevards define the planes below. Rather, a man stands in his house, sidewalks interweave on the streets; linking the two is a mental map or filter that alters the landscape, the slope of the hills, scales. . . . If everyone had a cartographer on call, pen in hand, he could represent his mental map on paper. Then we would watch as the geometry of the city's plazas shifts, as the distance between Plaza de Cibeles and the Puerta del Sol extends or contracts, or how the population density of Africa or the area of China or the altitude of the Parque del Retiro increases. With a cartographer at his disposal, Sergio Prim would have discovered angles like the paper cuts inflicted by a sheet of paper folded again and again, for he was fully aware that there were cracks in his mental map through which one might venture. But how might one gain access to the mental maps of others? How might one indicate these cracks on those maps?

My research was advancing slowly and you were gaining ground. One rainy Thursday, you uttered that fateful phrase: "I love you," you said, and suddenly time was running out. Not enough time to dodge the omen of your declaration. Under the eves in Plaza San Ildefonso, I touch my finger to your lips. Quiet, quiet, my dear geographer. Every "I love you" subtracts a second of life from the scarce seconds allotted the lover's fiction. Indifferently you stuck out your hand to see if the downpour had ended. Ignoring the catastrophe that had just been unleashed, you stuck your hands in my pockets. Shivering, you let me embrace you. Brezo, I thought, if only I could behave as if you hadn't spoken those words. Every "I love you" holds a promise and promises hurt us, for they divide life into moments of loyalty and moments of betrayal. I say "I love you" and I unleash your fantasy. If a piece of straw can become a beam in someone else's eye, a small promise can turn into a great omen of joy that is accompanied by fraud, the seed of resentment for what is said and not fulfilled. And who could fulfill it? No one, no one at all. Lovers, Brezo, are not, as Shakespeare might have said, the monster with two backs or even the phoenix that is reborn from its own ashes; lovers are the beast that consumes itself. Love self-destructs, not to assure its survival but to assure that it is lived: not like the grain that falls to earth and produces the ear of wheat but like the rocket that burns in the sky and in burning, lives and surrenders to death.

You gave me a push and we ran for my doorway, Brezo, you and your damp hair. "I adore you," you exclaimed—oh, imprudent woman—before kissing me in the elevator. Desire came, a stubborn, naked angel. Your back rolled to and fro, and I'm sure I told you that you looked like a boy, like a stream of water, and in it that stream of all of the bodies and faces I had ever asked for. Sergio was sinking to the depths, you were losing yourself, and inside me was the sound of shells strung on threads, hanging in the air and shaken by the wind.

But that didn't seem to satisfy you. There are wandering spirits that suddenly grow nostalgic, longing to arrive home and find the lights on: you were one of these. After we got dressed, you were back in your routine, asking where I kept my glasses and plates or how to turn on my stereo. You were forgetful, produced impeccable gestures: your hand passes over my forehead and I feel better, and this event can recur forever and ever.

Ladies and gentlemen, a man discovers a stag on his threshold. Now he embraces it in desperation. Do you wonder if he is mistaken? My life, Brezo, was full of approximate numbers. I would get lost in my addition tables, would cross things out in vain: our mistakes never cease to haunt us. On one side was Sergio, who kept losing rooks, pawns, castles, on the other was reality, whole and thirsty. It was the time you came up to my apartment, stood on the balcony, and let me stroke you on the side like a bird. I could have avoided your presence from the very start. I could have kept to myself: Sergio, master of his own scarcity. But I stretched out my hand and touched the stag. I accepted the serious interference you were producing, trusting that the only thing I owned, my secret, ordered intimacy, this silent point of rest, would extend like a jutting peninsula, like the bank of a river or the bulwark no one has ever attacked, so many attackers, conquistadors of an unwritten fate that is now a practically completed page.

21

My diminished output had not escaped the eye of Elena Morales. One day she called me to ask about the status of the report. I offered lame excuses, invented vague setbacks that had arisen in analyzing of the data, and even, given doña Elena's warm manner, went so far as to mention my emotional crisis. Indeed, she too seemed concerned. As I was saying goodbye, "goodnight" slipped out—an accident or perhaps my way of shifting into the penumbra, into the landscape of dreams and the unexpected. Doña Elena hadn't noticed. Turning away with an absent look on her face, she lit a cigarette and stared into space.

I gathered myself together at my desk, victim of a decision with no way out. Where should I go—to what kingdom of repealed walls might I bring you?

"Brezo," you heard me say at the other end of the line, "just as road maps bear symbols indicating lodging places, sanctuaries, and scenic overlooks, couldn't we mark our mental maps to show every point, light switch, crank, or ashtray groove where one might rest?"

"I think you're obsessed with a foolish idea." Your voice was muted by a dense irascibility.

What about the geographers of perception, I mumbled, and

Berkeley, the philosophical bishop for whom the table at which he wrote was nothing but a invention of the mind? What about the margeen, my friend, and your space bar? I don't know when you interrupted our conversation to say "rubbish." A woman's insolence, resorting to the same epithet my mother used to banish desire. But I didn't grow sad.

Communicate is such a feeble verb, I thought. One fine day our beloved confesses to us that on that blue afternoon while we were taking a stroll under the arbor we had said something that moves her to this day, but we no longer can remember what it was we had said nor even that the afternoon had been blue, but rather, that the afternoon had been faded and our comments banal. Such mental discord—oh, don't give me that sullen look—can also lead to treacherous attention: engrossed in a blush of confessions, who hasn't had the other person make some shrewd tactical move—sliding an ashtray away from the edge of the table toward the middle, raising one's hand to call the waiter, indicating with a slight jutting of the chin that our sleeve is about to dip into the soup. These and other sophisms instilled terror in my irrational and gullible youth. With a neophyte's intransigence, I assumed that gestures always corresponded to feelings, that what was said would be a precise reproduction of the underlying message. But over time we grow kinder toward ourselves. When you coolly replied "Rubbish," I was forced to consider that in emotions, as in the world of significations, there is a deep structure and a surface structure. To say "Give me the glass" is not the same as saying "Place the concave, clear vessel in my hand," though in some ways it is. And Sergio believed that in the deep structure of your heart, you understood him. A pause in space, Brezo, that is all I wanted. Stopping space and requesting a hollow, a resting place in which to pass the time with you without making any mistakes. How could you not want that too as you embraced me?

Strings of absurdities besieged our hearts, scores of pearly pebbles hammered us. You crazy woman, how could you not want to find a safe place, how could you not accept the fact that I was using time and the slight momentum I had to secure a territory for both of us? I would explore, sticking my arms into the void if that's what it would take to flee from the woman with the long kidskin gloves and pearl bracelet.

But finding myself stripped of clear and unassailable arguments, I hung up the phone, disconcerted. I did not find peace in the mechanics of my workload or in my lofty research. I returned home crestfallen. Sergio was a man standing at the end of a dead-end street. Sergio, odious Sergio, was accepting a gift given by a yielding, ardent, obliging, flexible, excitingly docile Brezo, then denying his thirst for company, his yearning to sit in the dining room in the afternoon, watching the rain fall. Why in the world do you love me? What in the world can I give you that can't be corrupted? A crystal paperweight on which dust has accumulated, a key ring of darkened or tarnished little fish, a stained tablecloth, an old sweater, a poster. They inhabit our house, Brezo, they are the sediment of the city where we lived at the time, far away, spangled with cliffs and domes. The long trips through the villages to reach the capital and there the opera with its chandeliers, thirty days of Austrian—or perhaps Norwegian—light dwell in that dusty crystal egg, in that empty box of chocolates. And memory? Memory, of course, remains. We can still refer to the differing thicknesses of the paving stones, the surprising height of the trees, but all we can touch is the souvenir, that disparaged symbol. When passion ends, Brezo, it retreats into objects—articles of clothing, gifts, letters. And if one is not familiar with the hollow, the channel that connects objects, then an object is just an object, a sort of carcass. May my passion never retreat, my friend, may my passion flow through a white space free from reality, along this oblong route I now am tracing.

22

So I stopped calling Brezo. Like someone dodging blame, like someone inhabiting what is about to take place, for he has learned that when dreams come true they cause pain. I stopped calling her because there are people who can exist day in and day out, but most of us can't. There are a few people who are perennials, but pine needles terrify me, that obligatory permanence, the inability to wrap oneself in reddish, chestnut-hued clothes and, like a man falling into a swimming pool, take one step forward, slip free of one's own mass. Sergio of the dry leaves, Sergio in hibernation lived in what was about to take place. And it was a peaceful there. During that time my juices would start to flow when I went outside, I could see the shapes of the air more clearly and perspective were sharper, because going outside often implied the prospect of bumping into her, even when a previous piece of information—Brezo was continuing to leave me messages—refuted this possibility. You will say that this is a cautious form of beauty, but what harm can there be in being cautious when we are already starting to grow old. On the other hand, I confess to you, my readers, that as I returned to my apartment, a headwind often made the walk difficult, my knees sinking as if crashing through layers of snow.

Until the day I answered the phone again and she stubbornly announced that she was coming to visit. If you only knew how scared I got of her hungry eyes and her proposals. The moment the nightingale or the swallow sings the man in love has precious little time to appear to be someone else. Sergio had precious few days to emulate the strange, teetotaling, amorous man people had come to see in him. When you called that Friday, a peaceful sun was touching the armchair where Sergio was reading, and it was as if he could foretell calamities and rain and lacked the strength to stay under cover. Sheltered and Brezo-less, what a contradiction. I agreed to the visit, to your presence, to the conversations that would later fill the house without fail like dust on the topmost shelves. I sat on the sofa, you lay down, and I clutched your forearms with my broad hands, pinning them there, quieting them there. Brezo, if you only understood: in those moments I felt as balanced as a plumb line—me, that bowl of pure instability.

As we undressed, you asked worriedly about our life together. Waking up in the winter and not seeing the enemy lines of the edge of the bed but rather, a warm torso, the outline of borders protected like a coast, something like that. Why would it ever have to end, you said. I didn't answer but brushed my fingers across your lips. I loved that contact. To possess a body is more than just soaring with the beloved—exhausting all the pleasure it can give us—and it is more than keeping the senses wide open. To possess a body is to actually take it, to know that its skin and organs are ours. The man is suddenly endowed with a pair of breasts. The man suddenly notes the inward curve above his waist, his hair is a different color, his legs, earlobes, and lips are new. And the man no longer wants to do without them. Your allusions suggested to me uninterrupted possession. What torture it is to hold on to reason as desire intensifies.

Yet I kept my wits about me. Brezo, I argued, it is worth remembering the other side of the coin. And just as we appreciate the pauses in the speech given by a well-educated man, pauses borne like a burden—time spent at elementary school desks, their impeccable reading methods—so are we fascinated by the tenuous existence of the odd-numbered man, his talent for overcoming adversity, his determined nights. You came looking for me out of respect for those gifts, came to me for them on the afternoon wave of a white shirt. But oh, insatiable one, you have come desiring to know the man inside and out. Please permit me, my friend, to conceal the sharp edges of my recently clipped nails, my sorrow, my fear of choking on a cherry pit as day dawns.

You nodded your head yes but your hopeful gesture and your questions said no. "Do you have any photographs?" you asked. You expected me to take out the photo album. You wanted to see me standing in a courtyard, on a beach, in the house with my grandparents: the boy in knickers laughing as he holds his grandmother's hand, the swimmer, teeth chattering as he emerges from a sea of shadows, a tangle of hair, a surly face, the boy wishing they wouldn't take pictures of him. You looked at the photographs one by one, finding signs of the tribe. And as you looked at the pictures you seemed to say: I love all these people, even the one I never met, the one who couldn't reach the doorbell if he were standing on tiptoes, the one who broke the window and then lied and accused someone else, the one you hide from me.

We made soup together in a display of mutual cordiality. You handed me a saucepan, I scolded you for not keeping quiet. This is how a man rebels against everything he has lived through: he refines his gestures with a manic perfectionism, tries to believe that all those other times he was petty, intolerant, rude were just early drafts of the final work that he is now beginning. When I asked "Where are the napkins?" what I meant was: I will never get upset at you, I will hide myself away before I utter a harsh world. I will be friendly, brilliant, won't let myself make a single misstep. I will become an artist before I speak sharply. But the man knows he will move his hand again and ink or a large spot of grease will land on the sheet of paper, the translucent oval of clumsiness. And on his lips, two red hyphens will attest to the bite of regret.

When we finished, as you were helping me clear the table, you made brief stopovers: plate in hand you tried out the chairs, the sofa, the upholstered gray armchair. Then, after you left, I saw you spread out, your body in the hands of my imagination.

The time has come, I said, to conjure you up, to your distinct but always impermanent presence. Woman, you are the kingdom of Aragon, I am Castile, and there is no room for alliances. This has been the essence of my destiny: to be the point that gleams and then is lost in the lives of others. Think of me as a recorded song. Some women have me in their house on a cassette, they put me on, listen to me now and then. I stimulate their romantic feelings, prompt them to act out scenes from the movies or the crystalline moments of a poem. But until I find that hollow where I can rest— that is your hollow—I must remain alone and take my place in a familiar story: that of people who have renounced eternal pacts, the anguish brought on by so many compromises, accepting that the hours of the day are no longer united by a unique presence. They are filled with fragmentary presences, are lodging houses crowded with guests one week and empty the next.

In the wastepaper basket a crumpled bag crackled slowly, like fire. Mephistopheles, I said, come here. I will give my kingdom and my life for a place where a feeling of generosity has equal or greater weight than the inadequate act. Mephistopheles did not come, and your hair was the color of my furniture as I walked my fingers slowly along the edge of the table.

23

It was then just two weeks before Christmas. Madrid was breathing the cold air of winter when you took me to the ancient house of wild beasts. This was my childhood, you said, peering into the monkey pit or standing in front of the polar bear's cage, but in fact it was superstition that had brought us: we had gone there so you could recover your strength. Afterward, we stopped at a small, nameless bar, and I watched you drink beer as if you wanted to hide. "There ought to be a subject in high school called the inner guide to Marcus Aurelius," you said, opening at last. "If they offered classes in serenity no one would fall in love as outrageously and foolishly as I am now." Of course, I recall your words with precision, though you must have thought that I was rude and inattentive as I wondered whether you were familiar with Swann's tragedy. You might not have known that Swann succumbed to negativity, to negativity and jealousy. Brezo, don't you realize that my negativity is losing you? I am Swann's beloved, my name is Odette, I am the coarse lover who was denied. I will end up talking to you about television shows, about my vile afflictions, my exalted vanity. My astonishment at having you will pass and you will hear me disown the polar bears. Get away from me, Brezo. Do I have a need to pervert you? Must I press you into the shadows? You will make me desecrate everything—this happiness and its resting spot, our cordiality, everything—so that you might remain free, so that the new Swann can manifest himself in you, the skeptical, alert, discerning lover.

"Brezo, tell me about your old flames like lingering colds," I said, but you were not interested. I understood, I really did. You were weary after having conquered your pride to declare your love and what you wanted was a response. So I said—or did I, Brezo? Was I afraid of hurting you—let me tell you about Lucía. Lucía was an odd afternoon with almonds, what doctors call a physical complaint that fades with the passage of time. Lucía was a sudden need to resolve everything, betting the house without any cards, an item of faith. When I came home I would open the door and usually find her sitting there, lost in thought, her black hair spread out like a curtain. These were useless days, a time for losing patience with the voracious fate that turns us into untimely, unscrupulous people. Living with Lucía, I compulsively chased after disappearances, always wide of the mark. But not with you. Within this pleat of my life, Brezo, allow me to apply my method freely. You aren't so different from Lucía, nor am I so different from your old lovers. No one is *that* different. She, on the other hand, is always the same. With kidskin gloves on she pulls the strings, and the only way to elude her is to methodically fill the space with holes.

We walked to a street of sluggish pink streetlamps. "Where are you planning to spend Christmas?" you asked the man fleeing the family dinner, fleeing families themselves. While I searched for a proper response, I caught sight of our pursuer in the distance. With a clarity that contradicted the laws of perspective, the hem of her dress, her pearl bracelet, her smile that spread like a gong were all growing sharper. "I may be going on a business trip," I said, improvising clumsily. I was afraid of seeing the disappointment in your eyes, but you just turned your wrist to look at your watch. It was an elegant gesture. Your silence—no questions about the trip—was elegant and proud.

There you have it, ladies and gentlemen; that's the story. It wasn't our first conversation nor would it be the last. You may be thinking that it had some significance. Believe me, they were the labors of love lost, flickers of irretrievable love. A man and a woman walk down the street talking, leaving identical sidewalks in their wake. In complete contrast, that dialogue between the sun and a plant called photosynthesis produces elemental forms of happiness—petals, for example. And this unsent letter, this blank monologue—blank, Brezo, because it doesn't fire a shot, because it wounds only with its sharp edge—this silent dialogue between the vigorous green plant that is you and a setting sun at twilight that is I, drops white leaves in its wake, sheets of paper spread against the night like white lines on a highway.

24

Thirty spokes converge in the hub of a wheel,
but it is emptiness
that makes the wheel roll.

A bowl is formed of walls of clay,
but it is emptiness
that makes it usable.

Windows and door pierce the walls of a house,
but it is emptiness
that makes it inhabitable.

From Part XI of the *Tao Te Ching*

At the office, logged on to my computer, I diligently copied
and saved every line as if they too were part of the "impact matrix
for interaction identification," the first section of the airfield study.
A mild inattention to detail had been seeping through my professional walls like mold, a bluish-green carelessness, a seed of passive
resistance that surprised even me. I have always been a responsible
person. I have always envied those with the courage to hand in work

late because they know how to draw the chalk line between their own lives and the rest of the world. I met my commitments with exaggerated punctuality. The very idea that an unplanned event could prevent me from doing so would paralyze me with anxiety. To my surprise the unpardonable lateness of my study no longer concerned me during those last few days. I felt like a sluggish ship whose heavy ropes were being untied all around me. My colleagues were my coast, a stretch of land growing ever smaller in the distance.

I was pondering the misty color of my desk when doña Elena came over to flatter me. The client, she said, had enthusiastically praised my earlier report on monasteries. "Good," I said, "good, good." I don't stutter, but misfortune causes me to get stuck on certain words. It is clumsy on my part and to describe this clumsiness would be immodest. Nevertheless, I wish to do so because that is where I glimpsed one facet of the hollow.

Take note, readers: I had intended to offer her a pleasant response but my gears got jammed. "Good, good, good, good," I said, and the more tongue-tied I got the more clearly I could sense Elena Morales's discomfort, something verging on shame. I tried to calm her down, make her laugh, but I only succeeded in increasing the number of "goods". I was receding, like a man dreaming he is sliding up a hill: "Good. Thank you very much," I managed to say. Doña Elena nodded and left. But in truth I was the one who had left first. During the ten seconds or more that I was aground on this shoal of words, I had vanished through an open door, a crack. Matter is not dense, as all of you know. There is space between the nucleus of an atom and the electron, between one molecule and another. Matter is discontinuous, like energy, and, according to some hypotheses, space and time are as well. According to this model, the years and centuries do not flow like a river but rather are a series of paving stones set one after another, molecules of space and molecules of time called topons and chronons. But what lies between one chronon and another, between one paving stone and another, between one "good" and another "good"? Clefts, gaps, the crack we avoid stepping on at all costs and through which I now wanted to slip.

I returned to my work. The military airport was planned for Alnedo, a town in the high mountains of Cuenca. And I, neither tourist nor traveler, decided I would spend Christmas in that town. It is not uncommon for one to lie and then find oneself obliged to turn these lies into reality. So I would go on a trip, as I had told Brezo. I was going, my friend, to the land of snow, cold, and the flu, to the disarray of a dicey hotel in a strange town. I was breaking my habits, making an exception. For whom? For you, for reality.

I walked home, the ashen sky giving off an odd glow. Remembering old airmail postcards, I imagined what Alnedo looked like: lads in britches, red-nosed and red-eared, standing in the plaza, streetlamps coming on, all the doors shut, and the whistle of gusting winds. Meanwhile, on my own sidewalk at the end of Calle del Pozo, a small girl held her mother's hand and tapped on the window of a pastry shop, her way of resisting this bleak time of day. What a frosty picture. When a city closes its confectioner's shops, it blocks access to the fantasy that lies at the source of all fantasies. Watch the little boy, his nose pressed against the store window. A stranger approaches. "Do you want that cake?" he says and nudges him gently into the richly colored scene. But it was that bleak time of day and I, a pleasant man, could never play the role of the magnanimous gentleman in this trite scenario. The steel blinds had fallen over the cream puffs, had sealed my decision with lock and key.

25

Saturday morning I bought the train ticket and made a reservation at a hotel in Alnedo called The Scarlet Ox. When I went to say goodbye to you that afternoon you opened the door with a finger pressed to your lips. You thought your father was sleeping but you should know that don Emilio, wearing a silk robe and slippers, was crossing the hallway, headed for the balcony. He had just enough time to see me abruptly break out of our embrace, my cheeks red.

We went into the living room. You crouched in a corner to make a phone call while your father, complicit in my flushed cheeks, pretended he was seeing me for the first time.

"May I speak with Jaime Orúe?"

I was startled, and don Emilio was observing the paleness of my face, so we both stood there in silence. You were oblivious. You spoke with infinite calm, without lowering your voice, entirely focused on one end of the thread, the other end being irrelevant. Hearing the measured tone of your voice, I had to acknowledge that a life, with all its laws and shadows, was passing by on the edge of my own. A different Brezo from the one who lavished attention on my telephones was coming into my view. You were no longer you, point-less woman, but a clearheaded character in Jaime Orúe's story—Jaime, the intruder, he who was making a mess of my bedroom, overturning the drawers of my memory.

"You know why my daughter has suddenly gotten interested in Euclid's precepts?" don Emilio asked me, at once curious and conciliatory.

"Jaime Orúe," I said to myself. I imagined you under his patronage: going to the movies with Jaime Orúe, taking him by the arm, displaying a self-assurance I didn't recognize. I could stand the wheel of bodies, the impending fantasy of your shared perversions, but not your calmness. You couldn't be Mild Brezo, Brezo With a Man. And furthermore, if your gestures were occurring in the company of another, should I see him or even be aware of him when I was lost in wonder at your contemplation?

"I have no idea," I said contritely.

"Don't worry, don't worry. It's after seven," don Emilio apologized, shaking my hand. "I'm sorry that I must leave the two of you by yourselves."

Feigning innocence, you opened a book and looked at me imploringly. But I was unable to concentrate. Without warning, reality had taken my imaginary tricks and was turning them against me: double-edged tricks. Brezo, my imaginary spectator, magistrate of my thoughts, held her own spectator's secrets, was escorted everywhere by a guard of virtual gentlemen, none of whom might be me.

"Do you ever have fantasies of simultaneity?" I asked, laying a trap for her. "By which I mean, do you ever find yourself sitting in the subway or a restaurant thinking that right then, at that very moment, that an enormous ship is docking in a Russian port, lights blazing on account of the fog?"

She had no such fantasies, ladies and gentlemen, she was untouched by our mutinous, phantasmagorical malady. And when

I reminded her of the first warning, "sometimes I imagine you," she barely reacted at all. I would be walking down the street and frequently would see myself walking down another street, a newspaper in my hand or sitting perhaps on a bench in the Plaza San Ildefonso. My silhouette would be floating next to her, but she never would have thought of doing a temporal reckoning. "That's what steady couples do," she said. "When I was at the Institute I'd do it: a friend and I would agree that at a certain time, wherever each of us was, we would hum the same song," she recalled, laughing, and her laughter frightened me. I wanted to tell her: Contain yourself a little, please contain yourself. Can't you see that although you guard against the feelings that undermine us and know how I loathe vulgar words, wool gloves, round tables draped in fabric, and glib melodies that I scorn and whose lyrics I tear apart and mock, can't you see that I'm faking it, that I'm a scrap of flag flapping in the night, sentimental and trembling?

"What do you want?" I said instead and went over to you.

You were thinking of an epigraph dedicated to the point: "The smallest possible dimensions, having no length, width, or depth." Perhaps that was the hollow, you suggested, a circle stripped of width. You were determined to adore me, you tolerated my obsession, you even consulted geometry textbooks to find ideas for me. Brezo, there are times in life when reason stuns and exhausts us and we must entrust our life to someone else, in whatever form, hand it over, deliver ourselves of it as we would a ticking bomb, black and round like in the cartoons. You loved me—begone, oh imprecise verbs—you came to meet me because you fervently wished to consent. Perhaps you had moved beyond the stage of resolutions and, having left it behind, felt no greater pleasure than that of yielding to abandon. Eventually you would tire of doing so.

"I am leaving for Cuenca tomorrow," I told you, gruffly. "I know, I know, I hate to travel. But I have to go."

"Tomorrow?"

"At two-thirty."

"I'll miss you," you concluded with a violent tenderness. My desperation grew in the shadow of the predictable expressions of emotion. Why do we appreciate those who leave more than those who stay? The organism grows sated and takes hours before it grows hungry again. We water a plant, the flowerpot is filled to capacity, water pools in the small dish and a day passes before it is slowly reabsorbed. Is that how our emotions work? Desire? Everything?

"Shall we go to my place?" I asked, nevertheless.

"I wish I could." As you sighed, the thread of pleasure you had been dangling was reeled in. You gave me weighty explanations: a matter that needed to be dealt with, a dinner at which the future of your work on the archipelago of the Baltic Sea would be discussed. . . . But now I can only evoke my sudden certainty that Brezo walled in by the large office table was Brezo forever clothed for what remained of the afternoon and for the never-ending week of my absence. We returned to geometry. I told you that I was somewhat disoriented in my research and confessed my timid intention—"What I really want is to try an experiment"—and even though your eyes were looking at me and your mouth was voicing relevant observations, your hand, stroking the edges of pencils, was not stroking me.

I dropped you off by taxi at the restaurant and was obliged to get out a few yards later. My desire for your body was thrashing me. Thrashing, just like blasts of wind, just like the light of your dress: illuminations calling me in my sternum, storm of desire that would not be placated, even if I straightened your body again from within, even if I possessed you again—how many more times would I have to possess you? It was cold, druggies were dealing your breath. They offered me hot chocolate, rubbed me down, but none could distract me. The forbidden body was coming toward me with terrible sweetness, filament within me, tombstone stretching beneath my naked foot, cloud above my head, my being entirely enveloped in pale light. I long for you, Brezo. I long for you, witch, slender woman, woman-girl with treacherous limbs, I long for you rhythmically, without pause, never forgetting for a moment that your merciless body is crossing the streets, riding elevators, settling in or stretching out without calling to me. I want to hear your body, dark and musical, pounding my desire, my desire orbiting your body, shadow and flame. Can you see it? Aren't you beset by the same assaults that stop me in the middle of the street and erupt in the night, that mountain of untrammeled pleasure, that trembling like a flower, like a petal destined to perish between the index finger and thumb of your hand?

26

An experiment consists of inducing a particular phenomenon so that one might study it. You, dear readers, are surely wondering how one induces a hollow. Brezo asked me that as well. Imagine, I told her, that today you hear that an old friend has returned whom you had long ago decided was lost forever to a distant continent. It's eight in the evening, you leave your house imagining the meeting, your happiness so irrepressible that you are laughing under your breath as you walk, because in the blink of an eye you have seen your past with that person and your future, the joy of being close. You board a bus, going down the list of places you are thinking of bringing your friend, arm raised, hand gripping the dirty metal pole. A man with a thick neck presses you against a woman's opulent bosom; she expresses her indignation with unmistakable gestures but you ignore them, focusing on the scene in your head. Your body throbs rejoicing as if you already were feeling the pressure of that first embrace against your ribs. But in fact it was all a false alarm. The person who had told you your friend was returning had mistaken the date or the name. "What a drag," some would say. Sergio Prim would say, "What a hollow." Where were you while you were planning this meeting? If you answer "on a bus," aren't you committing a sin of imprecision, to say the least? What was the emotion you were feeling composed of and where was it located: forty-five minutes of palpable happiness incited by an illusory event? The drag, though it hits hard, happens after the fact. It only affects the last minute, can't erase the other forty-four that have moved outside its jurisdiction. On the other hand, Brezo, to whom does that span of time, running counter to reality, belong? What category, Brezo, can we place it in?

27

Due to Brezo's haste and her appointment that evening, Saturday unraveled quickly, like a badly tied knot. I was up all night, seated in front of my ancient Olivetti. An insomniac glimpsing bats, I wrote and wrote. When the clock struck three in the morning I held a list of experiments in my hands. This was my earnest attempt never to say no, Brezo. Ever since you came to my apartment and let me caress you, I have sought not to make mistakes, to give you up but never to stop desiring you, to desire you but without succumbing to the monster of jealousy. To serve and adore you without becoming weak in your eyes, useless, foolish, and crestfallen, and so, unable to serve you. The hollow was my only option—to find it, to offer it to you on an altar of wobbly red wickerwork that was already waiting for me.

The train departed from a sleek platform made of dark cement. In days gone by the compartments emulated rooms, but not any longer. There are now entire cars without doors, row after row of seats, their backs facing one another. If it wasn't for the sudden rolling of the cars or the ribbon of rails that stretched into the distance, I would have thought I was in a delivery truck. That train had nothing reminiscent of accounts from the nineteenth century. A man who looked like a bible salesman tried to strike up a conversation:

"Are you from Cuenca?"

I gave him a curt "no." Luckily the uncomfortable position of our necks discouraged conversation. I kept up my reluctant monosyllabic responses until the man dropped his head and fell asleep. Twilight entered through the window the size of a movie screen: deciduous trees, old elms on either side of the tracks, bare black poplars lining the brooks, and on the hillsides the eternal parked bicycle with its lad commanding invisible regiments. But above all, I enjoyed the rectangular pastures and the land scattered in between. Looking at these fields I found the concept of area confirmed, believed in maps, understood that square miles separated one town from another, miles of open-ended land at all hours of the day or night. At this moment in time—take a look at your watch—one hundred nearly empty square miles separate Santa Cruz de la Zarza from Cuenca. Where population density is low, I thought to myself, perhaps bodies obey other laws: another form of gravity causes milk to pour into the bowl in slow motion, the law of entropy does not rule there, sex and night have other meanings.

We arrived in Cuenca somewhat late. I barely had enough time to catch the bus, and I took a taxi from the city to the town. The taxi driver said he knew The Scarlet Ox. Detached from the world I leaned my head against the window. Not only was I not appalled by the reckless speed with which the taxi driver took the curves, I was grateful for it, as it offered me a sort of rest. In fact, having life suspended in mid-air was a relief. Imagine, dear readers, all those decisions put off for later, the years, my continued survival placed in the hands of a village taxi driver and a chance truck on the other side of a sharp turn. We drove through the darkness with our highs beams on, cones of Brezo. I saw the movement of her body as she lay down in bed, propped her head on her hand, then sat up. Sergio recalled that gesture so its pinpoint of heat might spring forth in his hidden night.

"All right!" the taxi driver exclaimed, jamming on the brakes at the entrance to the hotel. I traversed six thick feet of open air, and, out of sorts, pushed the door open. Inside that large, ancient house, modern warmth awaited me. Enormous kettles enlivened the atmosphere, warmed the leather chairs, the slate floor, the metal tacks encrusting the ancient Castilian furniture, and the exposed brick of the walls. A pre-Raphaelite girl took my name, the waves of her blonde hair framing her face, ending just at the curve of her breasts. Her brother, I assumed, blond like her and with large, cruel blue irises, took me to my room on the left wing of the second floor. He left me there, sunk in the premature weariness produced by a travel bag at our feet and the crisply folded sheets of a freshly made bed. But before I had a chance to move, I was assaulted by a gust of incompatibility. The room was nearly empty: a bed, a night table, a negligible rug, and in the back, a small wooden bench with no cushion and a small table. In short, a bare cell, a thick cotton bedspread unraveling at the edges, a stone floor. And yet, what warmth.

The sound of the dark valley entered through the window, the wind snaking through the willow trees. There was a sound like the tapping of keyboards: it was the rain. I walked over to the window, that thin boundary separating the radiators from the world, the tangible room and the endless darkness outside. I am no longer a young man; I am too old to bend over and pound wedges with a sledgehammer, I loathe the menial work of brushing my teeth while squatting on the bank of a river. But I have not forgotten that the only night is that which transpires in the fertile, uninhabited wilderness. Water, crickets, and shadows. Contemplating that spectacle from my room was enough to revive my adolescence of absolutes. How I wished then that I had brought you with me, to look at the valleys together without a trace of anxiety. How I wished to embrace you as the thunder began, to witness the commotion of cumulonimbus clouds, a tremendous hailstorm.

At that moment I would have entered your room like a noise on the wind. But what can one do about distance? Large stretches of time for lips to touch. To go to your house and kiss you I would have to get into a vehicle, drive along the highways, obey the commands of the traffic lights. Or so Sergio imagined. I once had a friend who abhorred imagination: A bird cannot long to be a man, although I can long to be a bird. A bird does not suffer, but I do: it hurt. Unless—I ought to have responded—the man takes control of his imagination. Just as a bird flaps its wings, the man drives the car of his mind's eye. Night was falling and Sergio called you to him. Like someone throwing aside the drapes, crossing the chamber, entering the bedroom and looking at the bedspread, he is now looking at you. This is how I have walked through your dreams, have placed my hands on your shoulders, applying a fleeting pressure with which I take my leave of you, Brezo, my wonderment, so slightly joined to me.

28

I went down to dinner and found an oneiric object sitting on the tables that I hadn't seen since I was a child, on the first Sunday of every month at my grandparents' house. I am referring to porcelain soup tureens. The tureens at The Scarlet Ox were cream-colored and fluted, dotted with tiny roses. A tall, nearly bald gentleman was serving the first course on the menu. I chose the table in the corner, worried that some sociable lodger might want to join me. But there were only couples seated in groups of four, and they seemed to be in high spirits and self-sufficient. At the end of the meal, as though we were not customers but guests of an ancient duchess, we all moved into a drawing room with tapestries on the ceiling, sofas in abundance, and a fireplace that the boy with pale blue eyes was trying to light. Walls, cupboard, and doors plated with quicksilver, producing a telescopic environment of three-dimensional rectangles. I don't smoke so I lack the usual veil of smoke to stare at and to shield me from others. In order to assure myself of the harmless nature of my companions, I made use of a mildewed copy of the local newspaper. From behind its pages I watched and listened to them chatting to each other from one sofa to another. It appeared that someone—a woman—had suggested a nighttime stroll. The group was divided between those who didn't care for the harsh weather and those who were raring to go. I caught sight of the bald gentleman who was reclining on a sofa on the other side of the room, and engaged in conversation as if he were another one of the guests. When I finished reading the paper, I noticed how useful the polished quicksilver was. By means of a simple aligning of angles, I could stare at anyone I wished without that person experiencing any discomfort at all or even noticing my interest. I have always liked examining people's topographical features, catching them unawares as they rest their hands in a moment of inattention, their sonorous and pensive profile or their black moustache, their dark tragedy. The nape of the bald gentleman's neck nearly filled the frame of one of the mirrors, and there I laid my gaze.

Then I went up to my room and, after flipping through the pages of a book that Brezo had lent me, I tried inserting that nape into the hypothesis proposed by Saint Clement of Alexandria: "If the properties and dimensions of a body are abstracted, a point remains defined by a position. If one strips that point of its position, one finds the underlying unity" (*Stromata*). Abstracted from its owner and position, that nape became my antechamber to essential unity—a somewhat pompous expression, perhaps, but one that by definition indicated a particular region of the world equivalent to the hollow. When a man sets—or shall we say, settles—his gaze on the nape of another, it might be said that he has come to rest, as it were, perched on an inaccessible ledge or that he is, perhaps, reclining outside the clamor, inhaling the effluvium from the loops of a hookah. I sought my unity—the cylindrical ice-cream cone of your neck—in the bedroom, but all I found was a thick weariness in my knees, yawns without end, drowsiness that came like a black knight, visor shut, lance raised: the drowsiness of childhood, plump and round, so different from the skinny, elusive little man that is the drowsiness of the city.

I woke with the anguish one feels the day before Christmas, though I was relieved to know that I was in a sober mountain town, far from the shameless festivities. I found myself thinking of Lucía, who was also outside Madrid: "I'm going to the Canary Islands with some friends." I imagined her with her back to me, her dark mane of hair covering her shoulder blades and contrasting with her sky-blue silk pajamas. I imagined that if, as I opened the cap of a tube of toothpaste, I turned my hand at just the right speed, it might have an effect on her hand, causing it to raise the blinds on a terrace from which one could see the Atlantic Ocean. But Lucía had surely gotten rid of those pajamas, a gift from a friend of hers who had been in Japan, and was wearing another pair I did not know. A rough calculation verified that I had spent the same number of hours in Lucía's life as that article of clothing brought back from the Orient. The man who examines his own love is like the merchant who sells perishable foods. Shortly after meeting her, I had watched Lucía go into the water on a beach with some friends. Her nimble, confident movements, her skill at entering a group captivated me. And what has become of the shiver I'd felt at that moment? I vividly recalled that tingling from my days with Lucía, how the nearness of her neck during a simple peck on the cheek when we met would press a lever of elation inside me. I remembered this, but what human strength would have been required to press that same inner lever had Lucía suddenly walked through the door? Or in other words, what human strength would it take to contain my jubilation, my fierce desire to embrace her if, as I came out of the bathroom, I found Brezo waiting there for me, sitting in a chair, opening a newspaper, radiant, with a look of amused seriousness on her face?

Brezo, I could not avoid seeing you in a succession of scenes so vivid they ended up obstructing my partly shaved face in the mirror and thus, indirectly, you would cut me without intending to. I came out of the bathroom. No one was waiting for me. No one had come to surprise me. I opened the shutters, and an unfamiliar sun filled the room. Outside the willows were trembling, a dense white light bounced off the bare edges of the poplar trees and the distant frost. When a man contemplates the sea he finds it easier to be alone, and that valley full of willows resembled the sea. Your pacified absence joined the chorus of minor sensations that were being offered to me: imperial colors—garnet, cinnabar, ochre—an invasion of calm, agoraphilia.

Later that day I took a stroll through the town. There were no cars, not a single television voice issued through the thick walls of the houses; only the occasional cry of a lad calling to his friend or the barking of a dog cut through the air without doing it any harm. When I looked down the streets, instead of seeing more streets—the dirty stew of urban hives—I saw the meaning of the word distant. I lingered in the wide angles of the countryside. How near the boundaries of a town, how easy the passage from inside to outside or vice-versa. At the foot of an ash tree I tallied the expanse and its many names, stalks of lavender, thyme, the holly-lined path that led across the mountain. A sudden darkness distracted me: the span of a vulture crossing in front of the sun. I heard the rustling of branches, was enveloped in the scent of savine, lime trees, the inescapable scent of heather as clouds disfigured the day. I walked back to the hotel. Like any highland town in winter, Alnedo appeared uninhabited at three in the afternoon. And as I walked through the town, the collar of my overcoat turned up, I felt a romantic chill suffuse my body, the sort of chill that makes one long for a woman looking out the window while you are standing in the same bedroom. You approach her from behind and press your chest against her back, wrap your arms around her shoulders, and kiss her, though you have no idea what to say next.

An extravagant dinner in bad taste was approaching, topped off by turkey and champagne. When I entered the drawing room, the bald gentleman quickly came to see if I intended to join them. "Thank you very much, but tonight I wish to study," I said, savoring my state of absolute freedom. "Would you be so kind as to send up some fried eggs, a banana, and a glass of milk around nine?" I lay down on my bed, lighted the lamp on the night table, and reviewed my list of experiments. It began with several lines from *Ada, or Ardor*: "Not the recurrent beats of the rhythm but the gap between two such beats, the gray gap between black beats: the Tender Interval. The regular throb itself merely brings back the miserable idea of measurement, but in between, something like true Time lurks. How can I extract it from its soft hollow? The rhythm should be neither too slow nor too fast. One beat per minute is already far beyond my sense of succession and five oscillations per second make a hopeless blur. The ample rhythm causes Time to dissolve, the rapid one crowds it out. Give me, say, three seconds, then I can do both: perceive the rhythm and probe the interval." My dear Van Veen, how grateful I am for your hypotheses. First you decided to locate the gray hollow between the black notes, and it was as though a genius were doing the fieldwork instead of me. Once you had collected that data, identified the positions, you then would approach the object of your study as if it were a chalice from which you would extract that mystical substance: Time. Then I would appear in my overcoat, with the hands of a timid magician. "Please, would you let me live inside your chalice?" I would ask. For I'm not interested in plumbing the interval but rather inhabiting it, spending minutes or months of my life inside it, being its guardian, saying, "Let's pitch a tent," saying, "Freeze, instant," let me take a look at you, remember you: you are so beautiful.

In addition to these effects, the particular attraction of Nabokov's text lay in its specificity. The commentaries I had found up to that point were too philosophical, too insubstantial. In contrast, Mr. Veen not only used numbers, he proposed to delve into the rhythm. I looked around the spare, warm room and was inspired by the swaying of the curtains. I needed a pendulum. I took off a shoelace and tied it to my heavy wristwatch, then hung it from the wall lamp that extended over the table. Now I had to set its rate of oscillation. According to Van Veen, one beat per minute was too short while five beats per second was too long. I had to play with the length of the cord and the force of my tiny thrusts before I obtained an intermediate rhythm of three beats per second. It was hard to regulate the watch, for it was the only one I had, and I was using it as my pendulum. Nevertheless, by watching carefully and twisting my spine I was able to determine its precise speed. And there it was: an oscillation of three seconds. Was that the intermittent opening where the Interval began? Was it the vestibule, the doorway, the elevator to the hollow? I couldn't help but think of hypnotists: what if their profession consisted in revealing hollows? I rejected that thought immediately. No one had been trained in the art of remaining entranced as I had and I knew full well that this was not sufficient. A hypnotic state was not enough to avoid the traps of reality. Know this, dear readers, I sought the ultimate camouflage: he who looks at a bird and all but becomes that bird; he who reads a book and witnesses the miracle that in the space between his eyes and the civil servant in the stolen overcoat, the words are erased. He who is having sex and knows that outside, the world is dissolving. But sex requires passion, youth, vigor, an absence of stomachaches. My hollow, on the other hand, would be light and free of hazards, as easy as pressing a hotel doorbell: the palm of a hand presses a spring, the mallet taps the chime, someone answers the door.

"Come in," I said, and the pre-Raphaelite girl entered.

"Here's your dinner, Mr. Prim," she said, setting a tray right under the pendulum. It was a sampler of symmetries: fried eggs, a banana, and a glass of milk. "Are you sure you don't want a glass of champagne, some marzipan, or a few slices of nougat?"

"Now that you mention it, I would like to ask you for something."

I begged her to sit in front of my homemade pendulum and watch it while I watched her. Her features took on a golden patina, a mixture of skin and light, but no other noteworthy phenomenon took place. Tell me, my girl, what are you thinking as you watch that fan of air? Her answer was distressingly predictable: the next day a friend of hers was throwing a party in her house. The girl had agreed to supply music from the hotel and—this is what she was thinking—she still hadn't asked her father for permission to go. But wasn't I seeking a hollow as simple, pure, and fundamental as a chemical element? Why then blind myself with a hypnotist's elaborate tricks? I attempted to rationalize the situation by asking the girl a few technical questions—Did she see several watches or one blurry one? Could she read the time on the watch as it moved?—and then I let her go.

"Merry Christmas, thank you so much, good night, good night."

Sergio Prim, I said to myself, you have lost your composure. Without any consideration for her duties you have steamrolled this girl into compliance, forcing her to waste her time on a stupid triviality, and you didn't even apologize to her. That was when I blushed. I looked around the room for evidence: a pair of high-heeled shoes tossed under the bed, traces of perfume, pearls, a parasol. There was nothing. And yet, I had no doubt that I had been the victim of a typical joke played by that woman whose smile spreads like a gong. I went over to the window, expecting to see the model's gloved hands resting on the steering wheel of a car or her back in a low-cut dress next to a bottle and two glasses of whiskey on a wide billboard. Outside—I had already forgotten—were nothing but sinuous willows, scattered trees and overhead, like a splattering of paint from a wet brush, stars. I automatically thought, "Brezo, if only you could see this." So I called her.

Yes, I called you, for men are fickle and vanity—the desire to please—is powerful.

"Are you eating dinner?" I asked, afraid I was calling at a bad time. But Sergio's voice was received with a rush of surprise and laughter, and I made out a faint but heartfelt "I'm so glad you called." Everything amused you: the nape of the gentleman's neck, the pendulum, my Christmas dinner, white and yellow like Mondrian. As we talked I imagined our bodies pressing against one another, intertwined among the willows. And, as in those moments when we see the sky in three dimensions—the spherical moon, the stars on multiple planes—suddenly there was silence, and I perceived our bodies in that bas-relief scene, in the Milky Way, at the mercy of space, in the vastness of space more powerful than time.

When I hung up I went to the window and looked out. I felt reenergized and absurd as a schoolboy. I imagined Brezo looking out the window too, watching over her fleet of blue trucks. Are we that slight? Is our weight on the scale so imperceptible that all it takes is the image of Brezo, worn out and smiling, to tip today's pans? Companionship purred through my night like a car engine, accompanying my passage with the steady hum of happiness. I closed my eyes. Her elbows, resting on the windowsill, shuddered, causing the sides of her blouse to shake; her hair, gathered in a bun, revealed the nape of her neck; your profile turned to look at me.

My dear friends, I must beg your forgiveness once again. Brezo has barged in. I know I'm not giving you the attention you deserve, oh mendacious gentlemen in flight, velvet girls, ladies, lonely men, my companions in lascivious, baroque, intimate introversion. But what are my options when I have never touched your oval faces, though my hands know their way around Brezo's oval face by heart? Shouldn't she barge in? You barge in and, along with you, my hope that you will read everything that happens to me, everything my voice was incapable of spelling out because that woman with her red parasol and pearly smile would show up, dissuading all of us introverts, and impair our accuracy.

30

The next morning my room was filled with the ringing of church bells from the river. They were striking nine, the gray chill of a cloudy day visible through the window. I saw it without having to feel it. A hospitable temperature prevailed from my feet up my body to the top of my turned-down sheets. Each time I blinked, a drowsy swell of pleasure flowed through me, intense relief of slaked thirst reaching one joint after another. The hollow, Brezo, must be a state similar to when we move under the blankets and outside it is cold but in the bed, one wriggles around like the air, brushed by a temperature just right, that is what the blood wanted and produced in dreams.

Sheaths of sunlight came through the window and my laziness vanished. The town called to me with those shining bodies that are not yet ours but which call to us: the houses with their stone walls crowding together, the delight of walking once more to the ends of streets and finding the horizon. After breakfast I ventured onto the perpetual terrace, the circular boundary of Alnedo. And I caught a cold. The sedentary man changes his wardrobe too: I had gotten rid of my hiking boots, my down parka, and my raincoat years ago. At the time such clothing had a disturbing name:

hunting gear. But I soon decided they were excessively juvenile. And so I found myself fighting off the cold of the high mountains with just a padded mackintosh, navy blue on the outside, while the inside—due to some strange confusion on the part of the clothing manufacturers that was beyond my comprehension—was streaked with wavy pink stripes and tiny golfers. There were gaps between the coat's large buttons and the wind slipped through them as it did through the coat's wide sleeves and ample cut. By the time he got back to The Scarlet Ox, Sergio had the flu.

I asked for warm milk with cognac and entered the hall of mirrors. I felt an intense, almost unbearable pressure in my upper jaw by my temples. A lukewarm fog of unreality spread through my skull and skewered my thoughts. I lay in the armchair facing the fireplace, my hands and eyes focused on the steam rising from the milk. A gentle dizziness lifted me into the brilliant height of the clouds. While down below the fever waged its misty battle in my name, I glimpsed sunny expanses under blue skies. Thus I felt the humble benefits of mild illness: like dreams it allows one's perception to rest and relieves us of the pilot's burden. Slowly rocking to and fro, the bow and stern rise and fall inside me, a hungry splendor spreads, the word "destination" disappears.

The bald gentleman came to invite me to the special Christmas meal, but all I wanted was soup and some Tylenol, something sweet perhaps, and a blanket; and if it were possible, to have it all in front of the fire, right there in that armchair. No sooner had I asked than my wishes were granted. I ate, the blanket over my legs, the tray resting on the blanket. I sipped the coffee from a small tin mug that warmed my hands, and opened a book. Evening was approaching. From the room next door I heard snatches of songs that the girl was playing over and over again: polkas, habaneras, boleros. A tearful Anna Karenina had just sent a note to her lover and then, right away, a telegram. Sergio Prim was reading. The protagonist of a voluntary exile, Prim was obstructing the passing of the day. Letter by letter, character by character, Sergio was constructing an air chamber between time—his own—and Brezo's: a circuit whose pathways, spirals, and curves he traveled, free, relaxed, and out of reach. I have heard it said that there are people who can live for years without turning the last page of their favorite book: this is how they try to keep the miracle alive. I could never do that. Over and over again I felt helplessness, anguish as I watched the remaining pages growing thinner and thinner, while the pages lost grew ever thicker. And yet, I kept reading. That afternoon, however, Sergio granted himself a reprieve. I pried my gaze from the printed page, guided it through the air to the fire, and began to think about how the system that rules both the earth and its maps also rules men: scales and symbols, representation. Books are the maps of men. Every act of reading involves the paradoxical act of touching a map with the tip of the index finger and believing that we are traveling through France, moving through a chapter of a book as if we were climbing down the side of a mountain or ascending the cirque of a glacier by following its contour lines. I walk in maps, Brezo, I always have the street map of Madrid with me, like any tourist, for I believe in maps. They establish a unique relationship between us and the world, as do books.

But they come to an end. Nighttime was already suffusing the room. Every half hour a silhouette had come to poke the yule logs and here he was again. It was the young man who, when I returned, had taken my bags up to my room. Sometimes fate bestows us with blue eyes. Not all eyes are pale amber like Brezo's. Blue eyes, however, look just like prisms pierced by light. I looked at the boy and a slight ache made me shudder. I wanted to stay there, freeze the scene, capture his adolescent geometry in a single pose without, in doing so, giving him any cause for suspicion, annoyance at being watched, disgust at this ogling guest sick with the flu. So, let us immobilize this afternoon, let the hotel be still. Now, boy, let me look at your eyes, allow me the effusive warmth I feel as my eyes gaze into yours. Listen, young man. I am not the shameless boarder you think I am; I am Sergio Prim, a malnourished man with transparent eyes, hungering to look into your blue—or perhaps light amber—irises, eyes the color of walnuts.

He disappeared without even turning his head. I sat in a chair next to the picture window that looked onto the willow trees. Someone played a record of habaneras. Like a lamp, Brezo, like the corner a lamp forms in a dark bedroom, Sergio was thinking of you. You weren't there, but he continued to think of you. Surrounded by miniature streetlamps, he turned on the electric train that Father Christmas had brought for—could it be?—the bald gentleman's children. And the actress was waiting at the tiny train station. Beware of that figure, my friend, her tube skirt, her red parasol. Shun her, keep her at your back as I do.

31

The loneliness of the traveler, the loneliness I feel as a seeker of tunnels, thickened as I waited for aspirin at the counter in the bar. Brezo, I said to you, do you know the story of that man who discovered that all the swimming pools in the world were linked together in a single circuit? "That was when he realized that if he headed southeast he could swim all the way home. [. . .] He thought he could see, with a cartographer's eye, that line of swimming pools, that almost subterranean stream that arched through the county. He had made a discovery, a contribution to modern geography, and he would name it Lucinda, in honor of his wife." This is from "The Swimmer," a story I brought with me to give me strength. Oh, my friend, Baudelaire once said that men walk around bent double, each one carrying a chimera on his back. Its fabulous head crowns the men's foreheads like those horrible helmets ancient warriors wore to strike terror into their enemies. A curious detail: not one of these travelers seemed to resent the ferocious beast hanging around his neck. Brezo, pleasure of the spirit, incipient shift in space, see how I wish to lose myself in the words, in the stories of others, how I want to know that a man never—or almost never— lives where he is living. Sergio was at the bar of The Scarlet Ox, floating. He had gotten used to invoking your presence, but you should take care not to get any closer. Morose creatures roam the world, men unskilled at closeness, taciturn, somewhat dejected men, and if you disturb them it will result in discord. You will say I lack the necessary boldness to make a commitment, but would one say that birds lack the necessary boldness to run, that the mole lacks the necessary boldness to bear the light? Day wants night to follow, the forest wants squirrels to climb to the top of the trees, but the pine cones fall to the forest's floor. And there are men, hands clasped behind their backs, who when they were young, stood on the side at parties or played the records. While everyone danced they would admire their physiques. They are men who wear overcoats, and one can often find them standing quietly in a field, staring at an animal's burrow—either to imitate it or to guard it.

My cautious zeal collapsed altogether when I got up to my room and heard the telephone ring, a blaze of handbells. Clouds of cognac and medication under Sergio's feet, enveloping his head of dark curls. Brezo let out a hello! that sounded just like the messages she would leave on my machine. There have been no disasters, no unexpected events, she just wanted to say hello. I thought I heard the rustle of her shoes slipping from her instep. If only I could see you now. See you but not touch you, for I am weak, the flu is expanding like a column of smoke in my veins, my hands are on fire. But leave it to lovers to inspire compassion. I silenced my tribulations out of pride. What could I tell her? My friends, we love subtle connections, the organ concert performed in a German church and simultaneously broadcast in Málaga. I only needed to look at the knob on the radio by the nightstand to perk up. "Brezo," I said, "be careful. At any moment I might appear under your chin or come into your kitchen through the refrigerator door. You have stored my voice in tiny holes, and I'm letting you know that I'm going to jump into a swimming pool even though it's winter because just as I was remembering that story of the swimmer who discovers a sort of intermittent river of swimming pools, you called. You navigated towns, crossed the countryside, climbed through the telephone wire to enter my room. Everything is connected. I put a ballpoint pen in my drawer and, like Alice's rabbit, the pen can appear in the Queen's garden. To connect a fax machine in an office is to detect and register its secret conduits. The electrical lines that cross the fields trace vague yet lofty paths men grope their way along as they seek to follow them. I flush the toilet and the water that gushes in comes from Huesca. I open the medicine cabinet in the bathroom and the Mercurochrome overlaps and compounds with another bottle in a bathroom in Santander. I turn on the television and men in Krakow appear, the plug of my table lamp is fed by the Douro, my floor is the ceiling of the apartment below. And if I get into my pajamas I may, perhaps, come out through the golden nightgown of your body, your body that borders mine when we have sex. And if I go to bed, the mattress is the earth the Indian threw himself on to hear you gallop. And if I close my eyes you open them, shuddering with pleasure. And if I fall asleep, the tributary of my dreams flows into the river where you sleep. Everything is connected," I said, and I could hear you laughing.

32

Thanks to the flu, I got four full days of vacation—a vacation from myself. The world revealed itself to that other man, the one convalescing. From the scarlet plain rose flocks of ducks, clouds at dusk. Moving in time with the storms, I wrapped myself in fiction. Brezo's eyes, naps, books all followed one another. It was a time when the books seemed real and life, life was happening somewhere else.

On December 30th, my fever abated and I went down to sit in my armchair before the fire. The mirrored door slowly yielded, letting in a cart bearing emblematic contents: the snack, that light, schooltime meal, a phrase that evokes bread and chocolate even when it stands for wine and ham or fruit or, as it did at that moment, tea and toast. I smiled at the pre-Raphaelite girl, trembling in my frailty. No one had called her, but in that hotel family-style treatment was offered the way landscape or facilities are elsewhere. I walked over to the tables, swathed in a blanket. I chose the table that was most out of the way. The wind whistled through the willow trees and I thought of Brezo. Facing the picture window that looked out on the valley, I emitted radiations, waves for the unreachable one. I had made her unreachable by placing miles between us: sweet and bitter miles like orange marmalade, her favorite marmalade, so she had said one afternoon in my apartment. Ever since then, I, with the excessive delicacy of helpless men, always kept a jar in my breakfast cabinet at her disposal. Outside, a restless wind blew. One could hear landslides in the distance, and I was slathering my square of bread with huge, orange, luminous waves. The hail grew stronger, I heard the rumblings of extensive avalanches and a crackle of lightning, but the glistening of the orange marmalade protected me. Full of confidence, I gazed at that transparent surface. It was a test: people go away but their gazes stay with us, feelings shift like bands of light but orange marmalade is immutable. I polished off my toast with relief for certain small acts, homages, that, when prolonged, turn into tiny landslides of the heart.

As the heat from the tea filled my limbs with warmth and well-being, I found myself growing impatient with the wasted days, at still not having collected data or eyewitness accounts that might reduce the extent of my madness. Can a man counter his beloved, not with a profession, a medal, a passion, but with a point in space? And if not, does it matter? To yield, to return to the fold of crazy lovers. Look at them: like sacrificed animals, their offal falls through the centuries. They die that the legend might survive. Look at them in their beds, wicked in their candor: they are formulating their desire never to return to the world of crude things, to drain a glass and die then and there: little do they know that this is exactly what will happen. The lover always dies and the man bristling with fantasies, the scholar, the simpleton, someone else who is and is not the same man, comes to take his place. Brezo, my friend, I have perished once, so accept the wisdom of my ways. I have conceived a point in space for you. Someone else in my shoes would have made you a home, would have spent his days saving for the gradual purchase of a house and its furnishings. But isn't it better, my friend, to go mad over nothing, over the leaf falling slowly through the air, over the pale cold, over the slightest thing?

33

I passed the young man with the cruel blue eyes on the stairs. His greeting justified my nostalgia: "See you tomorrow," he said, his remark a rupture of dissolution. Except for the rectangular wooden step on which I stood, the floor beneath my feet, the unsteady world was shutting off for the day. I had no idea whether Brezo was asleep or around or even whether she was still Brezo. Men mistrust paradoxes but, good heavens, does my table exist when no one is looking at it? And might I exist, I wondered, only because the bald gentleman standing in the doorway of the dining room is watching me, expecting—demanding?—that I take the next step. "Mind the gap": I spent my life afraid of plunging my foot between the platform and the subway car, aware of chasms, resisting the crossing—on hikes, for example, when I had to cross rivers by walking on tree trunks, I would get dizzy. There stood Prim, stock-still on a landing, precipices once again plunging between every section of air before him. Not Albania, not even the ancient and proud country of Albania—Sergio Prim was a town in Burgos after it's snowed, a region cut off from the world.

I took another step, made it to the next stair, then to my room, and in my room found the enemy arriving. They were all there inside the room, teaching me to say that life is hard, that they should hang a carpet of lilies, lifeless lilies, dried dahlias, while I try to come up with a reason to call you, with an apology that would allow me to say your name and ask you not to go. *Solus rex* on a game board covered with glittering squares, Sergio was pining for you. White then black, your discontinuous, adulterous appearance was like the intermittent beacon of a lighthouse. Beneath that starless sky, Prim was anointed by the freezing cold of the countryside, was afraid of losing you, afraid that if he closed his eyes, when he opened them you would no longer be Brezo swooning. That when he turned to look he would see that the kite string had slipped loose.

Doubt, that keen, inclement doubt that portends loneliness at night, makes the visionary suffer. But Sergio had to stand firm. My friend, I belong to an erroneous minority: we are undercover monks, skinny, sickly Atlases conquering an imaginary land. And while everyone else was chanting their praying and prayed the *kyrie* and praying *consolatrix afflictorum*, be sure that Sergio was asking: "Allow me, please, to protect Brezo from deception."

34

I went back, though sometimes I believe that I never left Alne-do, that I float above the slow willow trees, that nothing has happened yet, that reality, in her *attrezzo* of dates and glass beads, is a tiny figure made of sugar on the sponge cake served in the afternoon.

In Madrid, the tide of December 31st had ebbed, leaving flotsam in its wake: beer bottles, soggy sheets of paper, glass shavings. A trio of cars, always different and always the same, stood guard on the asphalt; Sergio Prim was the pedestrian. Over the course of one's life, moments arise when a man tells himself the truth: I will never be a great geographer; they are not going to ask me to give a talk. Or: I am old; I have the skin of an elephant. Or: the hollow is a fantasy, a totally useless figment of the imagination. Sitting on a bench, I told myself the truth: Sergio Prim, you have run out of excuses, you have returned from your journey without the discovery that would grant you another delay, the time you need to continue searching for your great excuse, your fever. The hollow does not exist, Sergio Prim, it is a metaphor.

True, I love metaphors. "Metaphors alone facilitate evasion and construct imaginary reefs between real things, the flowering of weightless islands," a famous Spaniard once said. I would have turned my hundred-and-twenty-watt eyes on you. "Brezo," I would have pleaded, "Let's hide in a metaphor. When the pain comes, when it presses its sharp blade against us and covers the windows, when offense and misfortune come, we shall hide, warm and curled in a fetal position, in a metaphor." But can I overcome your unyielding practicality? It is not true that women are made of some soft material—they are made of metal. Their waists look fragile, they sculpt the arcs of their eyebrows, they ask for protection: a mere façade. Hardness is measured on a scale that starts with talc and ends not with diamonds but with a woman's mind. Women ask for details or hugs and it seems as if they had lodged a grievance for an enormous sum. They love numbers. Ten years of closeness, five thousand hours of leaning her head on your shoulder, two hundred and fifty-five afternoons spent reading and watching the rain. Take a look, dear readers, at the letters that Brezo would leave on the table. What is a metaphor next to that?

Weary, nearly overcome by my thoughts, I went into a café and, as usual, hurried to a corner where I could hide next to the tinted glass. But there I found her high-heeled shoes and pearl bracelet waiting for me. Dangling from a post in the plaza, reality watched me and laughed. "You deserve the best," the hypocrite said, "new styles for winter," and her eyes seemed to turn to meet mine. Sergio, I thought, tell her. Tell Brezo you're not going to keep looking for something that doesn't exist. I imagined calling her: Brezo, if I weren't a skeptic, would you give it a try? What I mean is, would you come live with me, would you bring me hot milk with honey when I was sick with the flu, would we buy a single newspaper to read together in the pub in the morning?

No, you cunning, laughing lady, you cannot deceive me by brandishing your vibrant smile. Lady of cigarette holders and marble lips, don't seek my perdition: hold back, socialize—why do you tempt me with verbs as hard as stone when I still haven't found the Interval? Don't you know I can't bear that constant rubbing? My childhood spent, it is not for naught that I am still fascinated by remote-control cars. I prefer that wireless link when connecting to the world. The amount of energy and social skill required to deal with my peers tends to exhaust me. By mail, however, and even on the phone, my fate concealed but also out of fantasy and memory, I am able to establish soothing connections. Distance is conducive to kindness. I am someone who writes down the itineraries of friends who go on trips. If they travel to Peking, I listen to all the radio reports that mention China. I had settled on ethereal connections and dispatches from correspondents until Brezo showed up and I wanted contact with her. A gong sounded, reality laughed, new styles for winter. To free myself from her painted mouth, pinned to the upper corner of the sky, I left the café, my glass of beer half full.

At the entrance to the café was one of those vaguely monstrous, coin-operated kiddy cars or gigantic animals. On occasion a child will stick a coin in and the thing will gyrate obscenely. I stood there, disturbed by that vision: such an insolent color, so lacking in tact. And yet, in a sublime attempt to conquer you, to win you over to my way, I made myself stare at the plastic monster and stop the world. This is how, after calling you, I could bear the bad news: the doctor was coming to visit don Emilio that afternoon. We would not see each other until the evening.

I waited for her, ladies and gentlemen, my heart like a shirt hanging on the line, and I held on, and still she didn't come. Half an hour after our agreed-upon meeting time, she showed up at my apartment, looking worried. Closed-mouth and curt, she hardly said a word. "I can't stay long. My father's not doing well," was all she acknowledged before hugging me the way one might close a door, heading for oblivion. Sex accomplished its mission like a sudden squall, absence in the face of an imminent threat, light in the darkened gardens. Then Brezo fell asleep. With her head on my arm, I thought about how desire is unpredictable, to say the least. You moan without knowing when the next one will come, my friend, but oh, how Sergio is freed by their repetition.

Once we were dressed, the space became more complicated: should I position myself according to respect, intimacy, or inhibition? Offering you a cup of linden blossom tea seemed as dangerous as sitting you on the table or carrying you to the sofa. And you drew no boundaries, failed to indicate any neutral zones, places where I could love you as do certain cloudless skies, without making mistakes or causing harm, without blowing it in any way. To devote myself to your affection as to a discipline of prayer or the cultivation of an orchard, like he who chooses a time outside the tumult. There are cups on the tray with the most delicate handles, through the window one can see Japanese mountains rather than city blocks, the moon sparkles in a glass of water.

Brezo lay on the sofa and stiffened her lips to talk to me. Cynical as an old lover, I deployed my weapons, played at stripping her feelings bare. "Narcissism," he said, meaning, "I only fall in love with a Brezo who is in love." As he searched around for that image he broached relationships, judging himself capable of committing acts of madness just to hold on to her, just to remember that Brezo might exist, a Brezo he would not erase from his memory, a Brezo who was not unstable, was not agitated. Such was the case that if she lost heart, if one day outrage or anxiety overtook her, her love would wane: "At this moment," the cynical lady reiterated, "I am about to lose control, loathe your silence, become hysterical or burst into tears."

Where was my stage manager? Why was he nowhere to be found? Why wasn't he giving me my cue—a gesture or a single word? There are men, Brezo, who have the answers. Affectionate men who in situations like these venture two or three sentences and are so bold as to lovingly put you in a neck hold. All I had were good intentions, a blue magma welling up, the desire to get you out of there, take you up the chimney. Like one of Chagall's grooms, I would grab you and at once we would be way up in the sky, far away when I heard you talking about pain.

You should know, dear readers, that don Emilio had fainted on the day of New Year's Eve. When Brezo found him, he was lying on the floor in the hallway, dressed to the nines, elegant from head to toe. He looked comfortable, tried to convince her that he was verifying certain hypotheses regarding the effects of the height of buildings on the human body. She thought his madness was getting worse, but in fact he was lacking oxygen. Over dinner, he told stories of things that had taken place in Huelva, the city where he had met his wife. Before everyone had swallowed their twelve grapes, he took Brezo's hand and made her wave it, the way one does with little children to make them say goodbye to one another. Content, he leaned his head on the chair and fell asleep. The doctor had a bad premonition.

Poetry is never practical, Lautréamont raved in his delirium. Like a jerk I tried offering you a hollow, Brezo, a vanished world. I rode with you in the taxi to your house. "Everything is going to be fine," I said, feigning encouragement. Sergio was performing routines on the high wire. In fact, his words were at least as illusory as the invisible hollow, but you believed them. When we got out, I saw reality sitting in the back seat. Wearing her shiny stockings, she had been spying on us from the cover of a magazine.

35

"I'm now trying to put into practice a classic physics problem, the so-called 'two-body problem,'" don Emilio said, as he lay panting in the double bed. "It consists of determining the general movement of two masses attracted to each other by gravity. The solution to this problem, an elegant display of mathematics, was enormously important in the development of scientific thought. But don't you think, my friend, that it's high time to apply it to our thinking about love?" Brezo pretended to listen to him while she watched his respiration. A hanging bottle of blue oxygen presided over the scene. "You are a wise man, don Emilio!" I exclaimed, and I sounded convincing. I saw gratitude in your eyes but you had misconstrued me: I wasn't trying to cheer him up. I genuinely admired your father, and his lengthy commentaries had raised serious questions in my heart. The two-body problem: though certain words might manage to touch on sex, it remains the province of the flesh, one of the forms matter takes, an unassailable layer of skin. And there, in that province, I was dying. Why your body and mine, Brezo? How could my body lose itself in yours when no one was supposed to have loved me?

Don Emilio fell asleep shortly after the doctor arrived. I went out in search of strawberry-flavored cough syrup, leaving the three of you in that room high above the outskirts of Madrid. It took me a while to find the pharmacy, which was virtually hidden in a nook between two blocks. She was waiting for me with her perverse fluoride smile on the other side of the store window. She wore a pink suit jacket, was beautiful, and I was sure that if I looked at her for more than a minute, she would trap me, Sergio, that little moth knocking against the poster, against the pane of glass.

As I left the pharmacy the rain let loose. I brandished my umbrella like a sword and shield, and as I advanced, I felled thousands of drops. But by the time I got home, I had lost my vigor, my composure, my battle arms. Danger surrounded don Emilio's bed, visible as a mosquito net. Brezo told me that she was waiting for an ambulance, that her father had fallen into a coma and the doctor feared it was irreversible. I remember clumsily attempting to buckle the tiny belt of my umbrella, that cloth spiral that never comes together but, like my spirit, always turns away from the automatic latch; away, Brezo, from what you need.

36

After all the anguish at the hospital my house felt like a locked chest, like a pitch-black mine shaft. Ladies and gentlemen, it is hospital rooms, their doors ajar—like prison cells, like wheelchairs, like raging pain—that don't exist. I had left Brezo in one, slouched in an ugly white leather armchair where she had settled in for the night, covered by my overcoat.

Sergio Prim, you small, wretched man, go get drunk because you know nothing, are a good-for-nothing. Camouflaged by the sweet, thick taste of a glass of port, alcohol found me. It slid into my mouth the way someone might fall down a laundry chute. To be expelled, to suddenly find oneself on the street, searching for the curb, trying to sit on the sloping marble sills of shop windows, to embody, for just a minute or two, an eighteenth-century lady skilled at crying, the simple art of crying, a spot of crystal on the cheeks.

I leaned against the damp rim of a fountain and your hips came toward me. What might follow? What glances might follow, what exhaustion? But not then. At that moment, just to hear a voice that is your voice and to make our way through the night to your apartment. To latch onto your hips, standing there as operating tables or fantastic animals pass by, what does it matter? Passion is a clump of crackling branches, lungs among flowers, and as night drowns, I would grab onto your shoulders of talc as they crumbled apart. Feelings are so impractical.

Suppose there is a tunnel in those eyes; suppose I wished to languish there, the train ground to a halt. You can't hear me; a river of hospitals is carrying you away. I've counted three, five, seven, nine days within this mare of the night. You walk around and the air is, as they say, less breathable. You stand up and feel your stomach constrict and your hands dangle like weights, everything happens very slowly, and you find yourself in a cloudy day with no light. In the distance they are changing the furniture, changing the schedules, before you is a single, horizontal stage: your father's face pressed against the pillows. Talking to you is awkward; you hear a sandpapery cough again and again or hear nothing at all. And all I can think is that the mare must go, because a mare can't gallop forever across your back, can't go to sleep under your hands. Instead it comes at night, crushing the privets, chomping on red geraniums, overturning flowerpots. Then one day the ceremony of death is over and the mare is gone.

I accompanied Brezo on several occasions down the long hallways of the tenth floor. Under a pair of light green pajamas, don Emilio's ravaged body refused to give in. His head, lacking memory and strength, wandered through space like a well-flogged idealist, a Quixote battling no one at all. Don Emilio would howl and attack with the delirium of a warrior. His violence—remote, scarcely more than a huffing and puffing—left him drained. Brezo was completely devoted to him—that is to say, was dying little by little—she placed moist scented washcloths on his forehead, spoke to him as if he could understand her. She would suddenly pick up and leave then return without warning. Erosion of Brezo, Brezo growing thinner at the speed of tragedy. Overcast, unaware, as if emptied by a cyclone, she carried on with jittery eyes: a beast of prey, hunters everywhere. Seeing her so quiet, the rims of her transparent eyes gray, I was desperate to get her out of there: not out of the city, not out of the circular path between the hospital and any other place on the map. I planned with me—Baudelaire, Baudelaire—to take her out of this world.

When alone, I would argue with myself, employing felicitous phrases like "perpetual help" and "our lady of the abandoned." When alone, I could bear the knowledge that no man is a maiden, that maidens are figments of literature. I have no comfort to offer you, my friend. I scour the closets, rummage through my past and in books, imagine promises, but who can replace the things you wish you had done with your father and will not do.

Furthermore, as you all know, pain is not contagious, is not transferable. One doesn't experience someone else's suffering, only one's own. My suffering was to be deprived of Brezo for no discernible reason and my death, everyone's death, also inhabited don Emilio's hospital. If only I could figure out how to stop Brezo's affliction, just stop it. Whoever enters a hollow stops suffering I thought to myself, and that also the hollow could exist in one's mind. So I took on a task that humbled my pride, that heightened my fear until it acquired the character of a necessity:

to share my know-how, to put it to the test, to seek an expert as I would a book.

It was doña Elena who, with kind speed, provided me with that person: "I know a psychologist who specializes in flights of the mind." A wave concealed then revealed the customary stillness of her gestures. "She is discreet and quite intelligent," she added. And then, after a pause, "I know what I'm talking about." The only way I could think of thanking her for her confidence, after jotting down Maravillas Gaia's phone number on a yellow sticky note, was to shake her hand.

38

I called the psychologist the day of don Emilio's funeral. Haughty death had arrived, the guest of honor, the ultimate redeemer of deliriums, always the whore. Maravillas Gaia sounded friendly though cool on the phone. She gave me an appointment for the following Thursday. She did not inquire into my problem ("spatial disorders," I had told her, "and occasional hallucinations") but she was interested in my physical condition: appetite, childhood illnesses, tiredness, headaches. Given her insistence, it seemed best to exaggerate. I magnified the dimensions of my insomnia, the anxiety produced by my dreams. I turned a simple case of unease into a pathology. "Triangles," I said, "upside-down triangles make me dizzy: spinning tops, certain traffic lights, the bowl of wine glasses, the letter v, the low-cut back of a woman's dress."

I hung up and started walking to the funeral. The straw color of Brezo's hair was reiterated on the heads of various of her relatives: older men, unfamiliar cousins. Brezo's friends, or her old flames like lingering colds, clustered in bunches. A thick blue line of the dead physicist's former colleagues rounded out the retinue. Though I recognized a few classmates from our school, I hesitated to greet them, preferring to slip by unnoticed. During the ceremony

I also kept my distance from Brezo, not so much out of delicacy as from having discovered the unspoken truth: she was leaving. A woman in high-heeled shoes and long gloves was snatching her away from us, perhaps in a limousine. Pale Brezo looked like a wraith and neither the rouge painted on the women's cheeks nor the knots of friends nor the unrelenting grief of her family succeeded in introducing any color into her face, white as lace, into the lace-concealed figure who was vanishing before our eyes. Only once did I dare to slip my arm around her shoulder: her body slid away, leaving my arm to swim through the air on its own.

Without Brezo's presence, the funeral was that of a great man, the honorable, elderly don Emilio Varela, a renowned physicist who, at the age of fifty, had gone mad. Every day there is a need for groups of acquaintances, friends, and relatives, a heterogeneous group that pretends to close ranks, act as if it were erecting a barricade before the gateway of death. Men of all kinds are called, must leave their houses and gather in those lifeless cities known as cemeteries. Sergio Prim took his leave as soon as he had fulfilled his ancestral duty, for he knew where to find Brezo.

That afternoon I went to her house. The doorman told me with consternation of the endless stream of signed cards and telegrams, of the multitudinous synod of relatives that still gathered in apartment D on the eighth floor. Brezo was sitting next to a candle, smoking—the first time I had ever seen her smoke. Now and then she would observe the animated conversation of the group and nod at inappropriate moments. There were no free chairs so I made do with a footstool, sitting next to her. I kissed her cheek. She didn't move. Now and then she knocked ashes onto the saucer that held her cup of coffee. Once her sleeve caught the teaspoon and knocked it to the floor. There was an ashtray just a few inches away but her hand refused it. Brezo, I thought, it is crucial that the coffee cups keep their spoons, that nothing fall on the candles, and that the ashtray's original function be restored. But I will venture even further: if I come with a cigarette lighter and you add a pack of cigarettes, we should choose the point of optimal balance, the most harmonious angle. Don't take this as the demand of a madman but rather as a simple defense of will. It would seem that we are being tossed about, that we are tired, overcome by the black shoving of the coffin. It would seem that we are working eight hours a day for thirty years. It would seem that she instills horror in us with her high-heeled shoes, captivates us with her patent leather lips. In short, in would seem that we are her puppets, but pay heed: you are a queen, scented with perfume. You reign over all objects and cause your earrings to match your dark green skirt, you place the ashtray in such a way that its reflection hits and is reflected in the teacup's gilded handle. And at this very moment you may utter a word from the Baltics because you wish to, because it calms you to do so, or because of its dactylic stress. Brezo, you should listen to me, above all because she is now dressed in black.

But to offer advice one must risk making enormous blunders or causing offense. And when I looked at her harsh face, death ripping pages from the calendars in the bedrooms, I didn't dare. I forded the river of a superficial conversation in fits and starts: people, sheets of paper, a piece of practical advice, attempts to distract her, how is work going? Her monosyllables, ladies and gentlemen, scared me. I started in on a comedic speech but your eyes were dissolving, you were not looking, and I knew that the task at hand was to wear you out, to hold you in the tense groaning of the night until you overcame yourself and could begin to sob. Crying is a state that resembles the hollow in that it is a place one can visit. One starts to sob and it is as if one's lungs are in the thick of a damp forest. One breathes deeply when sobbing, it is warm and isolates us from the external world. And though sobbing cannot replace the hollow, because it is ostentatious and gives us away and because a loud, pathetic handkerchief inevitably follows, it frequently provides us with fragments of a productive truce. Which is why I didn't say "Calm down" when the sobbing came, but instead placed the tips of my fingers, five unsteady tips, on your arm. I am guessing that you didn't notice a thing.

39

If only there were procedures in place. If only there were a type of relationship configured like an underground stream and one woke up to find an undulating presence approaching one's bed, free of the ongoing strain of words, of the palpable gravity of the flesh, like a fever. Brezo, my sin of laziness, my sin of omission: where can one learn proper, outgoing behavior? I proposed that we take a stroll along the Río Manzanares on Sunday. It would be like the Thames, like the Seine, it would be like the Danube, Brezo; it would be, Brezo, like the estuary of the Tagus below the marbles of Lisbon, like paddle-boats on the Mississippi, like the great Nile. You declined. On Monday, it rained and before I had a chance to make a move, you had already initiated your retreat: "I'm tired," you said. "I'm going to lie down soon." But on Tuesday you called me to see if we could see each other. Ah, the inappropriate, rhetorical question of a woman.

I managed to drag you out of that house where despondency seeped from the walls. The wind picked up, chafing the tree trunks and cracking my fingertips. If I didn't try to caress you, it was to keep from scratching your skin. For you seemed made of translucent paper that a pebble or particularly rough fingers would scrape you if they brushed against your skin.

Why am I speaking to you? Can't you hear the roses? Can't you hear them falling—in Denmark, in Russia, in the city of Pontevedra? When the last rose falls oblivion will begin. When these pages come to an end it will be hard to keep the conversation alive, you will no longer hear me. Brezo, if there exists a doctrine, if a place exists where men have defined a monologue, a dialogue, please tell them to come here. I want to know whether I am really talking to you or if I am like a radio left on in an empty house to scare away thieves.

Ladies and gentlemen, one morning an introverted man looks between his arms to discover that the stag he was embracing has fled from his life.

Now observe the exact moment when the stag began flailing about, struggling, craning its neck, eyes opened wide, in notable contrast to me.

Brezo walked past the bus stop and the entrance to the subway, a woman in a daze. Her large coat and small feet were quickly disappearing from sight. The harsh wind preceded her along the desolate route of her neighborhood: enormous avenues without a single tree, a single park, a single arcade. At that moment my perception was the only thing holding up the buildings: not another living soul was looking at them. Brezo was walking down the street, consumed by worry. An insolent weakness, you were already leaving the outskirts behind. Where are you taking me? She didn't say a word. At one point a traffic light approached us as we waited. How can I take care of you, madwoman? How can I take care of you when you silently place your hands on your temples, eliminating the world around you?

When she reached Calle Bravo Murillo her pace slowed. She rested against the post of a traffic light and then, reeling, about to faint, she leaned against me. Enslavement. As teenagers we read about it in poems, but never experience it in our youth. It made me shudder as I received her weight and the scent of heather at the nape of her neck. The supreme dictatorship of that body that ordered me around just by existing. With the stiffness of a dog on a leash, Prim responded to the nearness of her body. Aroused, I embraced her, my soul mate. It was her, would have been her regardless, and I always would have found her, even in another country, another year, another language. Sergio kissed the blue circles under her eyes. Objects began to scatter the moment I placed my hands on her neck: sidewalks, telephone booths, rearview mirrors all got up and left. The day ended the way a river is interrupted by a waterfall, only to return with all of its dangers:

"Come on, Sergio, let's go far away," she said, about to faint.

We entered the nearest bar. We are given improbable roles to play: as a man, it was my job to raise her blood pressure. A large coffee, toast, a glass of orange juice, and a slice of the upside-down cake reflected in the mirror. Brezo was already recovering.

"Are we going to go?" she insisted stubbornly.

"First I must find the hollow," was my tragic reply.

Her icy gaze grew sharp, shattered, then fell on me, piercing like slivers of ice. She called me to order.

"I was serious."

I was too, my friend, I was too. Sometimes, Brezo, the subway, the rails are illuminated by a thread of light, a strip of light that heralds the arrival of the train. Soon we will hear it clearly as it approaches, soon it will appear. Although this only lasts a moment, it is a place, a fragment of the voluntary-involuntary present we will be needing.

"Look, Sergio," she said, bridled rage, sobbing, and pride resonating in her voice, "I have respected your pastime, until today."

She was leaving, a fleeting bird flying away, with words that I repeat to myself over again:

"I have too many deaths and now everyone looks to me like they might be next."

I wanted to take her hands in mine, say, please don't think, close your eyes, but she was fading away and vulnerable. I wanted to tell you, touch me, it's the only sure thing we have, but you were fading away. Gone.

Brezo, Sergio hazarded explanations in vain, you suddenly fill with emotion, and I don't notice. Blushing, you would transport me as over the surface of the waters, and I ask if you have heard of the mutating flies in Afghanistan. We must find the passage that leads from one person's actions to another's feelings: a sturdy span, not a seamless bridge, but a passable one made of solid granite. Hear me out, my friend. Do you want me to perform the ritual as well? Do you want me to ask you, "And what will we live on?" or "How will I bear my fear of you dying?" Do you really believe that among your many names, I might call you Brezo Who Might Die? Brezo, if only one never had to walk under scaffolding every day, if only one had never gone out on Friday nights and seen the trampled sweaters and the lone shoe lying on the curb.

"You will spend your whole life," she declared, "untying the knots you are tying yourself, looking for that hollow you have made up. And what use will it be to you?"

At that moment it might have been to my advantage to calm her down: stay here with me and we will look at the blue rhombus on the sugar packet as if it were far away, until it is far away.

"You're crazy," she muttered with newly minted scorn. Like a bleeding woman who doesn't move, who doesn't reach for the phone or seek help, Brezo declined to play.

A woman has left, a woman is going away, leaving us all alone. Her despondency is as strong as the undertows at the beach, and it is dragging her backward. The half-drunk glass of juice and a barely touched piece of cake speak of her lack of appetite, of her fragility. Brezo was disappearing. Leaning back against the seat, she stretched her arms out and rested her wrists on the table—the last remaining bridge. But they were slipping. Her eyes were clear, clearer, clearer than before. After a moment of silence she got up to go to the restroom and I watched the movie star put out her cigarette and follow her. Tall, head held high, she wrapped Brezo in her silk shawl. Afterward she refused to come to my apartment, did not even let me walk with her. Unappealable woman, final recourse of my life, tell me: why do people make decisions?

40

I had an appointment that afternoon at Maravillas Gaia's office, right next to Dehesa de la Villa. After crossing Madrid on foot, I entered the park and got lost. My appointment was approaching and I, unpunctual, moody, exhausted from climbing up and down hills, insignificant amid the shouting of children and the seesaws, I ascended El Cerro de los Locos, but all I could see was the cross of a church and a mountain range sliced into sheets of blue. The park was concealing only one of its many exits: the one that led to the psychologist's street. I tramped the capricious hillocks and gullies once more, Sergio in the clearings, Sergio worn out on the corner of the city. The sun created caverns between the pine trees and the bare ground, tunnels the color of bread whose presence comforted me. I decided to sit down and rest on a bench facing an area full of red slides, monkey bars, and mazes. A boy pumped a swing a few yards from where I sat and his movement back and forth was slowly winning me over. "I bet that boy is a pendulum," I said to myself. That boy was probably my pendulum and the interval described by the swing designated the door of what I wished to be. His jeans and blue parka rose and fell. He was a blond boy in no rush: my antonym. It will happen to you on occasion, Brezo. You will go to a park and will see a man sitting, watching a boy on a swing. That man is not his father but a stranger who can't manage his life and has ended up there. The boy pumps with his legs, the swing moves to and fro. When the swing is at its zenith, the overcoated shadow of the man passes under the inverted arch: no one notices.

And from the other side a voice calls out: Brezo, what shall I do with you, cloud of my past, now that you have turned yourself into a downpour and are drenching my clothing? I, Sergio-Penelope, wove dreams and then unraveled them by myself. That was when I saw you disembarking. There were your feet, there was your crew landing on the docks of my poor Ithaca. I am a depleted land. There are no brightly colored stones in my dark mines. Rosebushes spilled over the garden walls and tradesmen could be heard, slowly making their rounds: junk collectors, knife sharpeners, itinerant musicians. I am on the street, I have asked for a light, have inquired about Maravillas's address, have wondered: where might something be taking place that could be my justification? For Prim has committed errors but now he is hoping to accomplish great deeds. With a garland of great deeds in my hand, I took the bold step of ringing the bell. With a garland of hollows. Brezo—will you want to listen to me now?—when time passes and your face harangues you in the elevator mirror and you can't find refuge anywhere you will know that Sergio has consulted the encyclopedias, asked questions, measured spaces, cast lines until he reached a tangible feeling and entered with you into the forest of the night.

The boy's heels left a skier's tracks in the dirt. An *s* floated in the air, the drunken wobble of an empty swing.

154

When I found the street it looked so long I took a minibus. A drowsing youngster was wearing a set of headphones that, despite their small size, broke my uneasy solitude with their buzzing. As you now know, I managed to control myself and didn't snap them in two.

"Good afternoon," said the psychologist.

I had imagined her as big as her name, so her unusually tall, irregular build didn't surprise me. I politely kissed her hand and spoke with deliberate calm. It was the trick of a timid man. I have been unable to check my fantasies of failure or my fear of ridicule, typical of insecure people. I don't know how to master my soul, but I have learned to govern my body. During the first five hellish minutes when I've struck up a conversation with someone I don't know. I should, I've been told, try to speak slowly. That is how I spoke to her. Though she feigned interest in my treatise, initially she barely glanced at its contents, and I feared that in her heart of hearts she would brand it with that ridiculous and degrading term people used for the lesser human passions: *hobby*. You already know that she attended to me keenly. My words on the hollow had grabbed the shoulders of her dormant past and shaken them vigorously, but I was entirely unaware of this. When I mentioned Brezo's name, Maravillas Gaia sat up, hands trembling—or was I the one trembling? To calm myself down, I went over to the window and looked out, stared at the mottled pavement. She got out of a taxi parked at the curb in front of the building. Her parasol was open like an umbrella and her elegant high-heeled shoes squeaked in the rain.

"Have I told you that I'm being followed?" I warned Maravillas Gaia.

"Brezo?" she said after a few seconds.

"No," I responded curtly. "Brezo is leaving. Every day she vanishes a little more."

Determined to translate my jumbled obsessions into technical language—into common sense, she said, correcting me in a soft voice, she asked me more questions. Maravillas Gaia's eyes were blue, the color that manufacturers of fountain pen ink call "South Sea," and white streaks cut through her albino hair. Had it not been for her indiscriminate use of your name, Brezo, I think I would have enjoyed my conversation with her, but to hear her say "Brezo" and not lose my train of thought required that I maintain a distance that was simply too difficult for me. Your name on her lips did not name you; it was an act of insolence, a foolish remark, an unpardonable blunder. She said Brezo as if you were a woman climbing a set of stairs or suddenly getting off a bus.

"Please," I said, interrupting her, "speak to me of the memory of fingers." Maravillas smiled.

"Why don't you?" she said, giving me the floor with a turn of her wrist.

"Once in a while musicians forget a passage from a piece. They try to recall it in their head and can't. Nevertheless, their fingers remember the passage and move confidently over the keys. What if our bodies were vast conglomerates of memory, what if saying 'I love you' were the same as saying 'I remember you with my body'? You keep suggesting convenient and intentional frames of mind but desire is involuntary, like certain associations of the mind."

The sound of the rain in the background flattened my phrases, erasing the inflections of my desperation.

"Desire," I continued, "is an unbidden evocation. It responds to arithmetic and almost always irrational mechanisms. Brezo desires me. I make certain gestures that fall on the inner vertex of her ribs then spread outward in every direction. I desire her too. When I'm alone, I know how insignificant I am and fear I will saddle her with my trifles but when her body appears I am a god, I am—if you will allow me the metaphor—the man whose dreams pierce reality like an arrow and then fly away."

Maravillas crossed her hands on her desk with decisive professionalism. When she looked at me, the turquoise water in her eyes moved. Her bosom rose and fell. She pulled out a piece of paper from a desk drawer, rapidly jotted down some notes, and speaking deliberately, containing the pleasure she felt as she neared the bull's eye, asked her original question, that confused question straight from the turbid, fantasy-filled heads of blond women. As in the pitch-black darkness of high school confessionals, a tremulous voice used to urge me on, saying, "How many times?" so Maravillas Gaia, sitting in her orange chair, the fingertips of one hand pressed against the fingertips of the other, said, "And do you see any relationship between your treatise, your search for those points you call . . . 'hollows'. . . and your desire?"

As you can see, she thought I hadn't considered this. She

thought it hadn't occurred to me that the hollow was inside Brezo, that every woman possesses a hollow. I sincerely hope that none of you hold me in such low regard. You might have anticipated my resistance, my modesty when it comes to portraying the obvious—cavities in Brezo, the hollow of her collarbone, the intimate hollows of her sex, the dwelling places. That man lives out his life exposed to the elements, that he is a reclusive animal—Sergio Prim knew that too. An animal beneath the open sky in search of cavities in which he might take refuge. A creature for whom a conversation is not always enough, who needs instead to be inside the body that is listening to him. Among the features that characterize the male, *viz.* his voice or a certain distribution of body hair, is also his defenselessness. You used to cover me, Brezo, my body bare of trees would bloom in you. But my member is sluggish, an inconstant connection, an organ that flags so quickly and must flag in order to exist. Otherwise the hollow would have to manifest itself in a lasting form rather than a haphazard one, would have to be invulnerable to the flu, to fatigue, to an absence of bedding, a particular time, or an appropriate mood. I tried to explain this to Maravillas. Then the rain stopped falling

"Are you sure you're looking for a psychologist?" she asked me in that weary tone of someone who hears but doesn't believe the words her lover is speaking, words a previous lover might have uttered. She slid her middle finger across her cheek to her cheekbone and then held it there. Her streaked mane of hair hung straight down, her head was turned to one side, distant, pensive.

"I'm not exactly sure what I'm looking for," I confessed. "I thought you would know the name of my hollow." And its nature, I said to myself, and its homeland.

Maravillas Gaia tidied up her desk. She placed her pen in a

small tray, turned the page on her date book that corresponded, I guessed, to this day now over.

"I wouldn't dare to baptize it at this point," she said.

I wanted to respond somehow and raised my arms.

"Listen," I longed to say, "perhaps I lack nerve. I've pursued moderation, for I am a man of excess; I've sought balance, because I have none. I don't know how to silence the demons, the braggarts, the failed musicians living within me. They are intolerant, testy creatures, they get worked up and howl like dogs in the hopes that their owner will take them for a walk. Is there any way to establish some order? Is there somewhere I could go when they all rise up in rebellion? If you could only show me the geographic location of count-to-ten-and-be-quiet. Because sometimes looking at the fabric of an overcoat isn't enough. One would have to retreat into the wings as the curtains falls and recite the beginning of that poem, 'They will say that you are still at the balcony railing, staring at no one, crying.'"

"It's quite late," the psychologist said with a sigh. "Would you like to make an appointment for another session?"

I nodded, my eyes fixed on the book Maravillas Gaia was pulling from her bag. It was a biography of Ava Gardner: the pearl bracelet, her eyebrows drawn soft and fine, the black, translucent veil over her shoulders. It was a warning. Reality would arrive with its surprises to carry us off: more ailments, more deaths, Brezo's first heartless gesture, the chill of a room in a damp hotel. Reality would bring unexpected demands. Only in the hollow, only in the fissure of things that cross our path, would we be safe.

As I stepped out of the office onto the street, I saw my shadow rising. It was not the thick darkness of the night but my shadow projected by the streetlamps, my rebellious shadow sprawled on the sidewalk, grabbing me by the lapels. It had me in its hands and it was a gloomy day with a single motif repeating over and over: Brezo, scorning my hollow, Brezo, refusing to come to my apartment, Brezo vanishing.

When I got to my house the tiny light on my answering machine was not blinking. Brezo, my interlocutor, where are you? We must speak with all that is distant, with She Who Is Distant. We must dig tunnels through the air to her mouth. I woke at dawn, dreaming it was my birthday. Doña Elena filed in, carrying a cake on a tray, but instead of a cake she had an enormous wheel of Gruyère. And perhaps my dream was just one of those straightforward longings caused by insomnia. Do you all know the story? It seems that a baroness, responding to a comment made by a count, muttered, "What foolishness! That's like preferring the holes over the cheese." I have on occasion imagined myself in that scene: "As far as I'm concerned, Madame Baroness, I must tell you that without a doubt I prefer the holes." With a peal of laughter the baroness would lay bare the cleverness—that is to say, the obscenity—of my remark. Elegantly, solemnly, I would clarify: "When I say holes I am not referring only to those pleasant orifices that give rise to your complicity. I have in mind the mute lips of buttonholes, the hole—an invisible rectangle—a book leaves on the shelf, the cloister full of music contained in a bassoon. And I can say with absolute certainty that I prefer the airy interior of the Easter egg to its thin chocolate shell."

The image of the wheel of cheese followed me to the office like a superstitious thought: perhaps doña Elena could help me. In the lobby the natural light blended with light from the fluorescent lamps, creating an annoying, overly bright environment. My foolish beloved, where can you be? The faithful crank anchored my eyes. But I wanted more. As in a landslide I needed to detect the precise moment when the hollow opens up and let it swallow me. I needed to get out of here, get you out of here.

I pulled up my sleeve to look at the endless ticking of the second hand. It made more than ten revolutions before I decided to call doña Elena on the intercom. "This is Sergio Prim. I'd like to speak with you. It's in regard to . . ."—I didn't know what to call it— ". . . a personal matter." She told me she was free right then, that I should come to her office. Now watch Sergio opening drawers, watch him look under books and piles of paper, rummage through his desk. He isn't looking for pens, he's looking for boldness.

"Please come in," doña Elena said with a smile like a ripple on a pool of water. She got up and led me to a sofa with two matching chairs.

"Would you mind if we went to a café?" I pleaded.

She looked at her watch with kindness.

"I only have twenty minutes," she said, but compassion moved her to take her overcoat off the hook. "Is it about Maravillas Gaia? Are you unhappy with her?" she whispered to me as we waited for the elevator.

"Well . . ." I hesitated. "More likely she isn't happy with me." We left the building. By mutual consent we headed to a café with large rooms and sat at a right angle to avoid facing one another.

Doña Elena, boss of mine, answer me this: Where does the border lie between one's inner and one's outer life? Perhaps I was never taught how to cross that border. No one gave me exercises so I could learn to translate my imagination into real life. To write on the day what we had written on the pages of our notebook. No one paid any attention to me when I suggested in class that we write our compositions backwards.

"Whatever your pleasure," I heard her whisper, but it wasn't her speaking, it was the waiter.

"Coffee with cognac," I said. No one understood me. "Coffee with cognac," I said again, attempting to clear my voice and my horizon. I caught the waiter's profile in the mirror and behind him, doña Elena and Sergio Prim, the man who had dragged his boss to a café to speak to her about. . . . I gathered up my courage.

"Doña Elena, do you think it is possible for things to exist outside our mind?"

We appreciate when the person we are talking with laughs out of delight in our vision of the world, but you can't imagine how grateful I was at that moment for doña Elena's seriousness. She only asked, "Have you talked to Maravillas about that?"

"Not yet." But I had to hold off on my story, seeing doña Elena's state of abstraction. Her slow, watery eyes resembled two birds perched on the rim of her cup, drinking.

"Go on, go on," she encouraged me. How thin, how wounded doña Elena looked. As gaunt as Brezo and in her own way, just as alienated. It would have been unbecoming for a gentleman not to rush to her side. I devoted ten minutes to her highly esteemed Maravillas. Doña Elena perked up to the point of radiance. She asked me roundabout questions, inquired about the tiniest details, and in vain attempted to hide her curiosity. Venerable, sober, tranquil doña

Elena was as giddy as a fourteen-year-old girl. Outside the café she must have remembered what had prompted our talk, for she asked about me.

"Doña Elena, do you think it's possible to stop space?"

She stuck her hands in the pockets of her overcoat with its concealed buttons and elegant turndown collar.

"For example . . . ?"

With more than a little audacity, I described her previous state.

"For example, to stare at the rim of a cup and have porcelain circumferences, pauses, open up."

Doña Elena crossed the street without looking.

"Okay . . . I see what you mean . . ." she murmured, undaunted by the cars screeching to a halt as they caught sight of her. "Look, Sergio, sometimes I get lost in thought without realizing it. My friends tell me I look like a sphinx. And indeed I do feel something stopping. But I couldn't say whether it was space or my own life. However, the one thing I am sure of is that I can't control when that moment will occur."

As we approached the office, doña Elena put on her professional face.

"You will find out that Maravillas doesn't think the way I do," she said. "Given how dangerous the world of feelings is, I would be careful if I were you. Can anyone choose the melody that cheers him up, the climate that makes him sad? Can anyone, Sergio, no matter how hard he tries, resist the influence of someone who torments him all the while?"

By the time we entered the building, doña Elena's transformation was complete. She was becoming her old, efficient self, was asking me questions about my work. But I was still the seeker of hollows, the man constantly attentive to his feelings. I placed my gloomy bulk between the elevator door and the electric eye along with my reason for not accompanying her upstairs.

A gypsy was selling carnations on the corner of Avenida San Jerónimo. "Do you want a few sprigs of heather with that?" I heard her ask. Her customer, a large, whiny guy with a lengthy beard, bald on the top, did not object. He paid for his bouquet and left, gripping the knotty stems of his carnations with sprays of heather. An aimless wave of affection, a breeze that polished the surface of the sidewalks, the white cornices, and the bronze statues high above us polished the tarnished silver of my spirit as well. If Brezo had appeared at that moment—did I mention that her name meant "heather"?—I would have shouted out loud. Irrepressible and happy, I would have agreed to anything at all. Down corridors of sunlight, my hand dozing in the fragrant nape of her neck, I would have accompanied her to the street where she vanished to switch the order of the days and to reply in kind: Let's go, my friend.

But a man is alone with his feelings. And they—in the end, just sensations in his mind—are volatile, are diaphanous, fickle creatures, undulations that might possibly be useful for composing music but not for living. Feelings, Brezo, never care about the time or place where they arise. I can invite you to eat, my feelings for you at their peak, only for the setting to betray me. The waiters are rude, the clatter of plates is loud, the place smells of cabbage. And it isn't the right moment: you arrive with a cold and concerns from other days; you speak to me anxiously of trips abroad, of a forthcoming project. . . . And there I would be sitting, waiting for you, compliant and mysterious. I must hide my feelings. Like those old men who wrap leftover bread in napkins to take with them, I must take small steps when I leave the restaurant with my feelings in my pocket, nurture them by myself. I must unwrap them when no one is looking, stroke them at home, turn on the radio to keep them company. Brezo, man does not always find himself alone with his desire: sometimes there is a body. Nor does he always do his errands by himself. There are days on which a silhouette accompanies him as he enters stores, goes to buy the paper. Man is not always alone with his conversation, his nightly news, his nightmares, but feelings dance like electrons, like sparks in his brain without anyone having to say a word.

A woman bumps into me—Was she tall? Was she wearing a bracelet? Did any of you notice how she walked?—knocking the gust of sweetness out of me and bringing me back to the street. I turned onto a narrow street, looking for a bite to eat, though it wasn't food I was longing for but a hollow. To move toward Brezo through a series of empty spaces. At the first pub, in the shallow bowl of an ashtray, I discovered the straight, rigid edges of my bed after they have yielded, altered by Brezo's presence. That metal object became a resting place, the zenith of my wasted morning. At that moment reality came in, accompanied by the insolent click of high heels. I heard her from the shadowy depths of my table: she wanted to use the phone. "It's busted," a joyless *maître* replied gruffly as he looked through the lace curtains of the window. And I knew she would leave without even glancing at me, for Prim had hidden himself. Someone said he'd seen her crossing an undulating bridge of steel. She was looking for you, the wind tangling her curls, flapping the legs of her pants.

The next day, back at work—you weren't calling, I didn't dare—I was overcome by the power of the sun and by a profound disagreement between my body and my mind that leaves us smelling like a park, as if we were seventeen years old, when in fact we are forty. It was one of those spring days in winter that hurt like a punch below the belt, like being tripped when one is running all out. I stumbled. I searched in the meager television guide for a region where helplessness didn't reign, by which I mean a lovely film in black and white. I couldn't find a single one. They had left me all alone. Who? All of them, conspiring together, they all had left me alone without a single movie showing to watch. One must be connected, Brezo. Look at the antennas lining the roofs. We are social beings, helpless and ready to latch onto reruns. Luckily there are other networks. Recall, Brezo, lover of letters, amanuensis, the erratic network of the postal system, its ranks of mailboxes, empty and full. In that same vein, the network of desire with its crossed wires, the network of insomniacs, the network of the lovers of César Franck, the subtle network of points, fissures, and intervals that is the hollow, that blade of arrested spaces through which I move, heading toward you.

It was dusk, and when I turned on the light I could not deny the evidence: right under the lamp was the network of the telephone. A slight movement, tapping the buttons seven times, then recognizing your voice, that comforting sign of your face, taking your voice and using it to draw back the curtain that covered your window and guessing which room you shed today so I might be with you. I tend to see rooms glazed with tiny drops from the latest rainfall. I tend to think that you produce a space filled with bright light that surrounds you. But no one picked up. Where could you be? Where were you? Oh, how I longed to kiss your eyes as the night fell in pieces, shattering in every room.

The next morning I called your house as soon as I got to the office, but you still weren't there. You had vanished, triggering the feverish impulse of my fantasies. In my mind I saw you entering a convenience store and buying stamps. Then you caught the bus that passed by the Naval Museum. Letting you go, I took the next one. As Prim arrived you were leaving with your research director; the two of you entered a café. Prim stood outside and promptly imagined that you were talking about the future of your professional life. You were asking to return to Finland as soon as possible. I wanted to wave to you: "Wait! Don't say anything—give me a little more time." Oh, fugitive woman, how quiet Prim was, sitting in his office while you proliferated one request after another. Implacable Brezo, determined to do whatever you could to forget that withdrawn man, that gentleman longing for a rest.

I was startled by Enrique's voice, right next to me: "Doña Elena wants to see you." He left, and I didn't have time to determine whether the malice in his eyes was genuine.

Doña Elena was waiting for me.

"Mr. Prim, may I invite you out for a cup of coffee this afternoon—that is, if you aren't busy?" she said, without any preamble.

"Please don't misunderstand," she added gently. "There are a few things I know about Maravillas Gaia that might be of interest to you."

I was afraid that doña Elena had lost her characteristic discretion, her oriental reticence. She smiled.

"Please, don't misunderstand me. It's about those pauses in space you mentioned the other day."

Brezo, I wanted to spend all my free time looking for you. But where, how, if not through the hollow?

"I would be delighted. Thank you for taking the trouble," I said. We agreed to meet at eight that evening in a grill with a Russian name and red upholstered sofas.

A silent interval filled the space between the time I left work and when we were supposed to meet. Like a madman, I thought you were home but weren't answering the phone. Like a madman, I took a taxi—faster, faster—and rang your doorbell: the house was empty, no one answered the door.

Doña Elena arrived, punctual and exquisite. Her dark bun gleamed in the light of the small red lamps of the café. A blind man was playing the piano, and she wanted to sit near him. She ordered a small glass of vodka. I followed suit, moved by the way she surrendered her eyes to the objects around us, attentive, as if still perched on her small rocky island of missions to accomplish, followed by retreat.

And now, foolish woman, listen to what she said:

"What did Maravillas Gaia do when you spoke to her about stopping space?" she asked.

"Nothing particular as far as I can recall."

"She was stalling. Mara"—the nickname slipped off her tongue, dear doña Elena—"has devoted a number of years to the study of something like the perception of fault lines in space: moments when human beings lose the notion not of time but of space—in short, a sort of individual eclipse. In fact her dissertation was titled 'The Loss of Space in Frames of Reference: An Analysis of the Perception That One Is Disappearing.'"

Doña Elena bobbed her head to the rhythm of the piano. Her black eyes with tiny specks of blue were two dragonflies perching on the smoke of the cigarettes, on the golden tassels of the lamps. Such a strange night, Brezo. So, Prim was not alone: a woman by the name of Maravillas was searching for empty regions of memory, for passageways to open. But I was losing you, the hours were thickening as you moved out of reach and a thought like a chuckle of loneliness and vodka wounded me: if you go now, Brezo, if you leave feeling offended, we may never cross paths again. We will never again enter the same store at the same time, never go to the movies at the same time, you will never sit in a car waiting impatiently for my pedestrian feet. Brezo, my piano, you will fall mute and Madrid will be an infinite, doorless maze, and we will not cross paths again. I will wait in vain at the entrance to public places, will sit in vain by café doors, will visit parks, public gardens, bus stops in vain. In vain, all in vain: we will never see each other again and life will become a story by Cortázar. I will devote ten, a hundred, a thousand days to coincidence, but we will never cross paths again, not in the subway, not under the air, not in the body. Perhaps this is the confirmation you desired, my friend: hollows, passageways—what use are they to me now?

Doña Elena had told me a secret. Her fingernails lightly scratching the tablecloth belied her nervousness.

"I'm happy to hear that," I mumbled. "But why didn't the psychologist want to tell me herself?"

The piano player stopped playing.

"Perhaps she suspects," doña Elena said, hesitating, "she probably thinks that I sent you to tell me about her. It's been a long time since I last saw her, and once. . . . "

Doña Elena was blushing. I rushed to interrupt her.

"I understand. You don't have to explain."

She set down her glass down on the velvet tablecloth in silence.

"But I want to explain. Once, a month after we decided to break up, I did send someone. I asked a friend to go to her office and see if Mara was okay. I wasn't motivated by jealousy; I just wanted to know if she was okay. She was taking her dissertation too seriously. She was convinced that there were fissures in space, switches that turned the brain, the passions, even breathing on and off."

The piano started up again. Doña Elena's voice, in cheerful contrast to the music, sounded relaxed.

"I hope that what I've told you will help to dispel any suspicions you might have of such an outstanding woman."

Doña Elena finished the glass of ice water she was holding with both hands, then she finished herself. She paid the bill, walked me to a street downtown, and said goodbye. Her bun blended into the night, her light-colored suit blended into the trunks of the black poplars she was passing by, and her slight profile blended with the light drizzle that had begun to fall.

"Doña Elena?"

Someone was watching as they strolled to the other side of the river. Maravillas Gaia, tall and gesticulating, started to speak.

"Doña Elena, a man came to see me the other day who said he works in your office. He is quite an interesting case."

Doña Elena's dark bun gleamed with streaks of iridescent blue. Maravillas continued.

"He is looking for a hollow too. In his spare time he is trying—meticulously, systematically—to refute the links human beings habitually establish with their surroundings."

"And what did you suggest he do?"

"You know it isn't my job to give advice."

"So, tell me what you foresee for him."

"Great sorrow. Or . . . " The psychologist stopped walking.

"Or what?"

From her ungainly height, Maravillas looked at doña Elena's tiny feet, at her dainty waist, as if wrapped in a kimono, and her deep-blue eyes. That is, she gave her a meaningful glance and said, "Or great happiness."

All night long, Brezo, I climbed down pipes. All night long

I dreamed that you were slipping away from me, escaping down drainpipes. And yet, escape is a deceptive word. At times I think it describes an impossible action. To say escape is like saying: I walked from the third floor down to the fifth floor, I ate water, I closed the door to my room and then went in. All night long, Brezo, I thought that feelings existed in geographic form, that they have a position, length, and diameter like the pole in the subway car I could grab to keep from falling. But what is that ringing? Who is calling on the phone and now is not calling? Who has rung the doorbell—was it you? Are you coming? I've gone to open the door for you and no one was there: a threshold of fear, a doormat plunging into the abyss. So you're not coming after all? So, Brezo, are you never going to come? You're tired out. . . . And I'm coming to understand that yes, you've grown tired of my clumsiness, my shifting moods, my crankiness. But I don't understand what you are telling me. I can't grasp that you've grown tired of my search for the hollow, of the mission that is at once a great deed and the greatest of tributes. Nor can I grasp that you might imagine being with me without the existence of a duty-free zone, a calm and lucid point like a coastal town in October. We need a space, Brezo, no matter how small, we must rob an inch from the platinum yardstick, a grain from the hourglass.

It was seven in the morning, too early to go out looking for you. Too late not to spin around in circles—insomniac heart, tumult of heartbeats—or keep from speaking to you. If you could hear my train of thought, the path unwinding like a road, if I were to tell you this and that, all that is contradictory and indefinite, two, three, a hundred times, then, beautiful lady, nothing at all would happen. Because man is a creature who doesn't communicate well, who dies with his movie reel of feelings behind his forehead. How can he incorporate someone else's film into his own, into his fleeting destiny? He would need another lifetime, a new reel, a long shelf on which to put each of the things the other person knew, her embellishments, her forgeries. Then the act of loving one another would not be one of fusing. Loving one another tends to be nothing but organized disorder, Brezo, pure chance.

46

I got up, which was when . . . "it occurred to him that if he cut southeast he could swim all the way home." That was my hope, remember? That everything is connected. Telegrams, lectures, letters, a postcard telling me of your whereabouts. Faucets, dressers, spectra of light, the waves of cellular phones, radios, kilocycles, the voice of sockets, the breeze of frequencies.

"Come here, my friend." I was watching the trees in the street, the pollen of ideas infecting architects, writers, musicians from a range of countries. Ideas expand, Brezo. They take hold of men working in isolation, one in Sicily, another in Palma. Oh, if only at that moment the idea of Sergio thinking of you had entered your mind, if, absorbed in flight, you longed for a gesture, if the idea of a hug fell from one of your branches and, gliding through the air, came to rest in my outstretched arms.

Brezo, call me soon, or are you unaware that bodies that go for too long without being touched can pass through walls, turn into ghosts, flap their wings, emigrate like a sheet of paper caught in a strong wind? If on opening a trunk, if upon looking at a shadow on a wall, at a chipped patch, I found the hollow, would I find it in your hand? And if, emerging onto the gentle slope of your wrist, Sergio kissed you?

But I am holding my tongue. I'm done with words. The world wants proof, the flower preserved from the dream, the dinosaur. By and large the world detests rhetoric, mistrusts abstract verbs: remember, believe, think, imagine, fantasize, represent. Those extroverts who stun with their clarity don't pay any attention to imagination. The world and you, Brezo, who were in the world, were demanding action, were dealing with reality.

I made my way through the morning to see Maravillas Gaia. I did not have an appointment. The street was wintry, the breath of passersby condensed into sudden braids of cloud. Maravillas agreed to see me, though she was suspicious. That was when doña Elena's frank warning came in handy.

"In the name of an acquaintance of yours, I beg you not to mistrust me," I said. "I am only interested in the hollow."

Maravillas relented. She invited me to sit down and apologized. Prim, however, remained standing.

"Good manners, Maravillas, require a slowness I deplore at this particular moment. Show me the landing on the staircase of things, tell me how to get there so I can show it to Brezo—and I beg of you, do it soon."

"I am just a psychologist," she said. "I am interested in the ways consciousness takes flight. A few years ago I investigated its conduits: fault lines, 'hollows,' as you call them, nicks in frames of reference."

She looked at me and I thrust my shoulders forward in a stubborn gesture. Maravillas's voice brushed them as it passed by and her words sought to gather me in.

"I don't know very much. But what I do know is at your disposal."

What can I say about that interview, oh Brezo, loss of my faculties? What can I say about my impetuousness and my disappointments, my fluttering heartbeat as she enumerated her findings, the weary, somber torment I felt as I realized the extent of her doubts?

"When I was young," Maravillas said, "I wanted to specialize in anxiety. I was interested in the idea of a contemporary Polish psychiatrist, Andrzej Niewicz. In his view, states of anxiety are disagreements that patients are having with time. Let us observe, Niewicz says, the girl waiting for her boyfriend to call. Watch her walk to the refrigerator five, ten, twenty times to get a drink. If she were listening to music while she waited we would say that her inner clock is marching to the rhythm of the hours. But that is not what is taking place. By means of a compulsive series of senseless movements, the girl is refusing to follow the rhythm. Although the example appears to be a minor one, I will tell you that for Niewicz, seventy percent of lesser nervous disorders are explained by the specific chronometer of each patient.

"So, I had a dissertation project. Niewicz had invited me to work with him for the first few months of the semester. At the time

I was doing my doctoral courses, I was also setting up this office in which today you are my guest, Mr. Prim. Two days before my departure a gentleman arrived. (He was not so different from you: a little taller, his eyes a lighter shade of blue, no moustache.) An old acquaintance had given him my name. He took one look at me and he said, "You treat people who are having trouble with space and time." And before I could correct him, he added, "I'm having problems with space." He was a quiet man of Portuguese heritage named Julio Bernardo Silveria. I only saw him on four occasions, which of course I regret. I was fascinated by his case: he was experiencing, shall we say, moments (he preferred to call them states) of willed disappearance.

"I can see that my story is catching your interest, Mr. Prim. I won't try to describe those 'states' for you. At first I thought they were mere hallucinations. As you know, a hallucination is a perception that lacks an object. For example, seeing a seven-headed hydra when there is nothing but a hallway. A hallucination can also be the belief that one is in Burgos, gazing at the stepped gables of the Burgos cathedral instead of this lamp. Silveria, however, was not seeing things; he was experiencing partial memory loss. "I alter space," he explained. "If a star can do it, why can't I?" he said, revealing a vague knowledge of modern physics. Apparently huge stellar masses create a kind of depression in space. Julio Bernardo Silveria considered himself able to generate small dips in his immediate surroundings where he could hide from the world.

"Julio Bernardo Silveria." Every time the psychologist said his name I shuddered. It takes so little, Brezo, for the rooms I inhabit be filled with presences. Reality stood in a corner in the back of the room, tall, provocative, her black-gloved hands resting on her dress. In the other corner the ghost of Julio Bernardo Silveria paced about, intermittent, partly air, partly sheathed in a dark, shabby suit. He was wearing a fedora made of blue felt. Maravillas sat to his right, speaking to me. Facing her, sunk in an armchair, I listened to her, fearing that, as prescribed in childhood games, you were standing in the middle, my lymph, my brain, my heart. As in those cruel childhood games, you were in the middle, holding everything together, waiting for one of us to make a move. Four corners: someone has to move. They quickly switch places, and you, standing in the center, must also run. Brezo, I always found myself cornerless and now, when I'm finally going to get one, I am afraid of finding you in the middle, I am afraid that you have left, solitary one, and I cannot call you, cannot say, join me in this hollow. Might I be wrong? Could there be no empty corners, no empty countries? Could every conquest be a defeat?

"One fine day he stopped coming." As if she had noticed my distraction, Maravillas was speaking faster. "I haven't seen him since. But the data I obtained during those four sessions were enough to change my dissertation topic. I canceled my trip to Poland. My new research would focus on the rejection of space and the perception that one is disappearing. Professor Niewicz offered to work with me from his department. Together we formulated an original hypothesis. However, we had to interrupt our research when we got to the stage of carrying out our experiments. Try as we might, we couldn't find another subject who complained of the same pathology Silveria had. Six years have passed since these events took place, Mr. Prim. Six years and three months, until the day I answered the door and found you standing there, talking to me about your wish to go live on a crank."

Brezo, Brezo, how awfully disconcerted I felt, how suddenly I was overwhelmed by indecision. Maravillas asked permission to observe me. She promised to share the results of her speculations with me if I agreed to become her "test case." And meanwhile, you standing on train platforms, you adrift, madwoman, you, as if Prim didn't love you, as if he weren't dying to have a piece of you, as if he weren't trying to learn how to vanish just so he could love you better, Brezo, secret light, conscience of my darkness.

Hesitant, tenuous like the blue flame of a cigarette lighter in the sunlight, agreement emerged from my mouth. Maravillas Gaia absentmindedly fiddled with several paper clips, then let them drop. There was a tinkling of rounded edges, your presence, your transparent eyes watching us. The psychologist proposed an intensive schedule: Monday, Wednesday, and Friday from six to nine in that room full of ghosts. When I said "okay" a certain blue fedora swung back and forth atop the coat stand. We shook hands and as I left the office, Maravillas asked me to do an exercise.

"Watch every person you speak with. Make yourself look at him or her carefully for fifteen minutes without stopping, making sure that the person is there the whole time. When you report back to me, I want to hear that you didn't take your eyes off of any of them for even a second, when any of them might have disappeared."

What are you doing, Brezo? Shrugging your shoulders? Do you think Maravillas is a fanciful woman? No, please don't push the air with your hand. Submit as you would to a lullaby. Hear her explanations as if they were my lips on your streaming back:

"Our internal perception of our own existence is a discontinuous phenomenon. We only experience the feeling of being right here and now, reading a book, once in a while. The same is true of our awareness of the world. Why? The amount of sensory data that surrounds us is much greater than what we can assimilate. The slightest movement of our head produces a shift in perspective, and the shape and size of objects are altered. A fountain pen seen from one end would be nothing but a circle if our eye didn't insist on pretending to see a fountain pen. Within a radius of several hundred yards objects shrink in size as we move away from them, yet on occasion we assign them constant sizes. If we paid close attention to shades of light, we would notice countless degrees of luminosity that produce a shift in the color of any piece of fabric. Yet we say it's red. We are constantly making corrections—at times imperceptible ones—for the purpose of constituting the external world. We need to give our surroundings a (fictitious) permanence. This is the so-called realist perception, and there are those who consider it to be as inaccurate or false as types of illusions."

According to Maravillas, Julio Bernardo Silveria was applying these devices to his interactions with other people. People, she said, look at us discontinuously. Someone is with me now, he glances at my sweater, he glances at the expression on my face, then he designates me as the person with whom he is going to have a conversation. After three or four minutes, he may scarcely take another look at me, but in that interval his words were not addressed to me, exactly, but rather to the picture of me he has formed in his mind.

Silveria took to observing the frequency and manner in which such breaches in attention occurred. If he ever disappeared—however briefly—in public, he would take advantage of those intervals of discontinuity. In all other cases, when his interlocutor became aware of what he was doing, he would immediately discard the image, given that, as I explained to you, Brezo, we tend to correct for variations in our immediate environment.

My apprenticeship began with observation. I had to take responsibility for the table always being there and always set when no one but I is looking at it and it appears to be set. But you have vanished, and all I can see are your red nipples, your face with its gaunt cheeks, your heroic fainting spells, impatient woman, Brezo, who has been snatched away from me.

The wind escaped between the walls of the houses as I closed the door. It was raining green needles in the park in Dehesa de la Villa. The pine trees were shivering like willows, like a certain Sergio Prim venturing into dark undertakings, and all the while there was you.

48

A man comes home to his apartment, goes in, finds neither stag nor threshold, and thinks that the landscape of his street could easily belong to Ireland or Corsica, the way it floats adrift on an ocean that in turn is floating adrift on an ocean that. . . . Madrid had lost its bearings and was missing the periscope of a tower on whose eighth floor lamps were lighting, switched on by your hand. Like an elderly man I carried a chair over to the window to watch the rain. Brezo, I am the Minotaur and your return left me vulnerable. I was familiar with geometric loneliness: the two hundred and fifty-five streets, the six hundred and twelve street corners, the forty water tanks were all alone. I might have survived the fierce swords, the massive attacks of men, but not the demolished walls, the world outside, the light. My friend, my Ariadne, Theseus did not kill the Minotaur: it was you, it was your thread that led to the death of his labyrinth, to his own death. Because of your discretion no walls remained, no passageways, no crossroads. The elements lashed at me. Leagues stretching one after the other beyond the sea, men, arms colliding, brandishing torches, lighting their clothes on fire by accident. And the monster was dying. The Minotaur without his labyrinth is like those minerals that turn to liquid when they come in contact with the air. Find an urn. Find the bend where time and space come together and disappear. Brezo, Brezo, my Ariadne, how can I get you to understand that I need the hollow in order to serve you? And to disappear as if through a set of drapes when low pressure clouds my eyes and the rooms of my apartment, when I can no longer summon the strength, when common sense flees my temples and lichen howls in my stomach and darkness reigns in my breast and expanses of scorching, dead rocks cover my soul. These are the limits, Brezo, of the human condition: my head gouged by spurs or the final moment of my happiness, which sometimes falls on Wednesday. I take a step and can tell that my happiness is coming to an end, that it is reaching the border with Portugal and no longer exists, that it is crossing the Pyrenees and turning into a country of lime trees and the bell towers of churches, is the Norman gothic style or the inside of a casino. But what happens that Wednesday when I run out of happiness should you come and need me to be happy?

I barely had eaten a bite, for I was constantly watching, staring at the low glass table and the coaster with the picture of a Dutch windmill. This was my assignment: to keep watch, to determine whether they were staying put or if they sometimes hid themselves in a crack in space. I was on guard for new perceptions but didn't find any because I was looking at you. Like a coward, I loved you when I lost you and like a coward, I noticed your head resting on my shoulder.

My apartment burned itself out until it was dark. Brezo, Brezo, the birds swoop endlessly in circles, delineate useless vortices as if they were trying to fly above themselves. Where are you now, my friend, as the afternoon declares itself and I am a swift flying in circles like a madman? I would give it all up—let psychology crumble, let its experiments all fail, let me forget the hollow ever existed, and let me set off in pursuit of you. But reality places thistles under our pillows that scratch our faces. She is evil like the housekeeper with the keys in her hand, is powerful and cold and comes armed with her own plans. Where can I take you then?

I went back to work, still not knowing where to find you. I felt unable to show my face, to turn on the computer, even to accept the noise of an indifferent office and would have left, feigning a hangover or pain in my chest, had it not been for the quiet voice of doña Elena, her aura of calmness and complicity. With utmost discretion, slipping her question in among remarks about my report, she expressed her concern for my state of mind. We went to her office.

"I don't know what to do," I said. "Doña Elena, where does a woman flee to when she flees?"

Then I spoke to her of you. And you were no longer Brezo Denied but the way out of my banks of fog, "my human love." Doña Elena offered to help me find you.

"But what will I do if I find her?" exclaimed pale, ignorant, fainthearted Sergio Prim. "What are her dreams, doña Elena? When a woman looks out the window of my house and sends her gaze from one rooftop to another, what are her dreams? You are a sensible woman. Please don't talk to me about the things we already know are lies: eternal adoration, the invisible charm of normal life. Talk to me about dreams."

"Mr. Prim, I have dreamed about what you call normal life," she said and a weary sadness broke across her eyes.

"But that life doesn't exist," Sergio said, lowering his voice to keep from annoying doña Elena, to keep from annoying you, Brezo. "Reality puts containers full of dead yoghurt in the refrigerator, lets in cold gusts of air, makes the tables wobble, and causes the glasses to spill. That is when we dream. A man has dreams, doña Elena. A man is the place where imagination happens."

"When I was young, if this is what you're asking, I would imagine I had been kidnapped."

"And then what would happen?"

"Then," doña Elena said, smiling, "the Trojan War would start."

I could see her irony, large as the wings of a man hurling himself from a mountaintop, opening inside his apartment. Doña Elena did not wish to understand. Doña Elena joined you in telling me that after the dreams comes the succession of days. And what about the disaster, what about the sinking dead, the dying towns, the gray boats? What about all those boats, their bottoms sheared off? Could one live without stopping to listen to the overcrowded train that hurtles over a cliff in the Andes every week?

But I will tell you my dream, Brezo, my seer who left without saying where she was headed. I don't imagine afternoons or table-cloths, I imagine we are at peace, that the movie of your desires and the movie of what I lack have both stopped rolling. Because reality is like the horn of a car boxed in by a double-parked car, like the Walkman whose tapes a little boy replays endlessly and is never silent. But when a man stops, reality stops too. If a single man on a single morning stops rushing around, behold: a crack appears in the order of things. During the blurred years of my time as an architecture student, I learned a crucial concept, Brezo: the denting of the soul, that being the line of force that passes through the beams, where its solidity resides. If excessive pressure is applied to a beam, its soul is dented, resulting in a curvature along its length. The denting of the soul; in this barbaric region of time, perhaps the weak men are right: men who refuse to work with others, who live with a dented soul, who retreat, and continue to create pauses in space, curvatures that, when brought together, might give us a habitable sphere.

50

I wasn't sure whether to continue with Maravillas or go in search of you. But how might I search for you? Africa, Peru, Albania (even Albania), or a province of Spain (Zamora, for example), a house an old friend might have lent you. You could be anywhere.

If I went back to the psychologist it was not to forget you, my lodger, it was because of the dreams. Imagine cyclones in the middle of the street, imagine that I had been squinting out of incompetence, my eyes growing smaller and smaller. Rushed time, youth flown. My enthusiasm, my longing to live were leaving me, Brezo, and I would be forced to recite the world to you. And one winter morning you would ask me for apricots.

Maravillas received me, notebook in hand. This woman who had been so full of questions, so curious that first day, did not even ask about you. She spent the whole time taking notes, cold as the windowpanes.

"Are the hollows connected?" I pleaded nervously. Her albino hair wounded me like the sun in a mirror.

"We are examining the possibility that space can be altered. What do we need connectors for?"

But I wanted a tunnel, something that would connect my position with yours. Maravillas read my mind.

"When you learn to alter space, you will be able to get close to that friend of yours right away, simply"—and her glance made me shudder—"due to the fact that the word close has no scientific basis, it is a convention like the adverbial phrase 'far away' or the concept of distance."

The psychologist opened a small door and led me into a tiny room with a projector. The image of a plane in the form of a napkin appeared on the wall. It was the fable of the ant and the orange. Remember? Your father told it to us years ago when four or five friends had gone to your house to study. Place an orange on a napkin so the napkin curves inward toward the center. Put an ant near the orange. If the ant does not wish to climb a steep slope, it will start walking in concentric circles around the orange and in this manner will slowly climb out of the depression. The orange is the star that has curved space. The ant is a satellite in orbit around it.

Maravillas turned the projector off but left the room dark.

"Imagine," she said, "two points at opposite edges of a blank sheet of paper. Anyone would say that the points are far from one another, but that depends entirely on space, on the sheet of paper, on the napkin. If we remove the sheet of paper, two points remain, adrift. If we fold the sheet in half, the two points are superimposed on one another," she concluded, quickening the beat of my desire.

Brezo, what is the difference between knowing you have sat in this chair, which I can almost touch from my bed, or in another chair two hundred miles away? I now understand that the universe is a single path through the air, that at night space is joined, and through it my rails stretch toward you. Though you don't appear, though at this moment you don't appear, know that we are joined on an enormous plane, on a small sheet of paper. It looks like we are alone—Sergio in his room, you on a train platform somewhere—but a hand materializes and folds the paper in half.

51

When we left that wretched little room the hollow started to take on names. It might be called folding the sheet of space or shaking it so that our latitudes, Brezo, were expelled like motes of dust and mingled.

In the remaining minutes, Maravillas Gaia passed on the advice offered by Julio Bernardo Silveria. According to that man in the fedora who wanted to alter space or suppress it, one must first cultivate a state of calm.

"But how?" I sighed. Then something unbecoming occurred. Elena Morales called on the phone. She kept apologizing. It was about my report: Juan Peña had demanded that she give it to him within twenty-four hours. World of misfortune, reality was gripping doña Elena by the bun, stealing her serenity. I had to leave immediately. Maravillas had stopped in mid-sentence and my mind was in disarray. "The mystery of space, of distance may not exist, but who but a taxi driver could shorten the traffic lights for me," thought Sergio Prim. It wasn't Maravillas who transported me nor that man of Portuguese heritage, it was the taxi driver. And in the interim, you, Brezo, my prayer. What I wouldn't have given to know your whereabouts. If heartbeats were numbered, madwoman, if starting a relationship were like raising the taxi meter's flag, how high the sum of my heartbeats would climb, what a large tab I would ring up. I placed my heart in the pulsing of that machine but the taxi was arriving at its destination and I still am beating.

As I expected, the office was empty; there wasn't even a shaft of light coming from doña Elena's door. With deliberation and vague melancholy, I set about finishing the report. I worked for seven hours with their four hundred and twenty minutes without faltering, almost without getting up. I worked as I had in the early days, producing a report that was beautifully written, daring in its proposals, and judicious in its reasoning. Each indisputable conclusion was a leaf on the plant that the florist's shop never sent doña Elena as a token of my gratitude for the last few days and as a kind of farewell. And so I completed my last project at the office. Sergio Prim had decided to soothe his soul, to bring it to a halt, and to this end, he was leaving. From a distance, a somewhat tall gentleman called to me. A man in a fedora, blue as the sea, a man was beginning to direct my disappearance.

When my project was done, I leaned my head back and saw your hands. They were coming toward me from out of the blue. Perhaps they had caught boats, consulted flight schedules, or purchased train tickets, but they were your hands, Brezo, because hands travel and hide in specific segments of time, are transparent pillows. Then—how odd—the hollow opened up a bit. Your body drifts from one room to another, from one sofa to another and then another, the sofas, windows, and beds in my house multiply when I embrace you. So it is with the hollow: it resembles light, it drifts.

It was so late my colleagues would soon start arriving. The chill of dawn was condensing on the doorknob. My conjurer's hands longed for doors I could open with my gaze alone but physical contact was required. I placed my palm on the metal and it grew cold, and the cold was a white sword that passed through me. I placed my palm on the metal and knew that sometimes silence sounds like a shadow, is terror. But behind the terror is nothing but the day with its slanting suns. So I placed my palm on the metal and swore, Brezo, that in my concavity I would learn to love you. As if an equation had been solved, your hundred naked bodies let my hundred bodies rock them back and forth. I challenge the coming day, I said, and affirm that man must learn to live in the imaginary world. Just as man often talks to himself without speaking a word—for if he were to say all his thoughts aloud, he would produce an unpleasant linguistic commotion, would offend silence in its sacred manifestation—so too must he often exist without performing a single action—caressing, suffering, accompanying someone in one's imagination—and this is the essence of moderation or restraint, of gracious comportment toward you, my wave, my particle.

At the base of a pillar, reality, furious, flew into a rage. It wasn't true that I could leave her perfect shoes behind, her curves that sang in the night, the inverted triangle of her back. Reality stepped up her rage and sharp darts, black threats flew by me. But Brezo, a somewhat tall gentleman, wearing a fedora, blue as the sea, a creature with a "faint voice" was protecting me. I swear to you it's true.

52

I left the office as people headed toward theirs. In the subway, the bustle of people that had always rattled me and from which I fled took on the painful attraction of last things. They were the eight-in-the-morning commuters. I know them all, Brezo. I didn't used to look at them. I would avert my eyes from that mirror of loneliness, sweat, and decay. But now that I am planning on leaving, I am filled with nostalgia to see them for the last time. Their freshly washed faces, displaying an unseemly drowsiness, are etched in my memory.

When I came to the surface, a crushing green obscured the view from the subway entrance. With difficulty, as if I had to dodge a series of transparent screens that blocked my way, I made it to my doorstep. The never-ending job of holding ourselves up: we are bones made of calcium, sentimental stalks. I had dropped my wallet on the ground, was taking out my key when I saw you coming. What were you doing in my neighborhood at this time of day? Were you looking for me, Brezo? Were you looking for me? You had to get a sheet of poster board from the craft store near my house, you said. You were drawing the maps for your project. And yet, what maps could they be? I don't know why I believed you.

"Would you like," I said, then paused, my voice evaporating, "to get a cup of coffee?" I felt faint, like a man who'd been up all night. You couldn't stay long. Please, please, don't go, don't let geography swallow you again.

"Are you angry with me?" I asked.

"I think so," you said, hesitating.

Your nearly transparent eyes had grown larger, woman window. Sergio was vanquished by fear and sleep, but oh, how he wanted to look inside you. You were a crouching compulsion, a whirlwind of ideas spinning on your forehead. What were you hoping for? What were your desires? I took your hands in mine.

"Please, come up for five minutes."

The body gets the news and braces itself before the man finds out. Before I could glimpse the void or the vertigo I would feel, my stomach clenched up and a severed diver's breathing seared my lungs. Only afterward did my ears understand: you had accepted my invitation.

An ode to incongruity. Save for the state of my soul, for whose sake I found my ability to reason weakened or incapacitated, my thoughts smothered. Brezo, jar tipped over and spilled out, I had to touch you. The anxiety of desire, lips joining at their cornice, their outermost ledge. An ode to incontinence, to total abandonment, to the definitive blending of atoms, if this even exists and is of any use for expressing uninterrupted fusion, the disintegration of memory and the present. A passing train continues on its way. Yet experiences of pleasure are unique events. A short while later we were moving like two automobiles in adjacent lanes, alone, an orange ring of smoke periodically emerging from your mouth.

"I'm going back to Finland. I leave Sunday night. You still can come."

Brezo, Brezo, why do you come looking for me when my soul tends toward excess, toward spite? When I persist in bumping into my furniture as I grope my way through the room? When one doesn't know other people's point of view, what is going on for them, one experiences a sort of insecurity. From the point of view of my insecurity, I can't fathom how you could love me. It is as incomprehensible to me as an obscure text, an obscure meaning. Brezo, my friend, I was not trained to accompany you. Please, readers, be so kind as to explain this to her: How can a man who collects pauses, who seeks stillness, pick up and go?

I didn't reply but, draping my bathrobe around Brezo, led her to my desk.

"Sit down."

She smiled slightly. Though she barely could tolerate suggestions regarding the way she led her life, she liked to be led when it came to trivial matters. I brought over a pencil and a notepad and began draw space with its curved depression.

"Remember when your father explained this theory to us?"

She looked at me sternly: of course she remembered. Don Emilio's presence had covered her memory like a sheet of rain. She listened impatiently to the Portuguese man's thesis and rejected it out of hand as being pretentious and absurd.

"Only enormous masses can curve space. This man's ideas are nothing but a bunch of baloney."

The delicate moment had arrived.

"Julio Bernardo Silveria's hollow may not exist, but you will be relieved to know that someone else has been looking for it."

"You're nuts." And this time her pronouncement was conclusive.

Brezo, imagine that you could calm emotions when they

wash over you or swiftly expel certain tremors twisted by reason due to their resemblance to melancholy. To stay in those heartbeats as in a room, to feel their heat, to touch their inner laughter, that would be the hollow.

"I would like to take you to a hollow," I said, though she was retrieving her clothes and to watch her pull a stocking over her foot was to see the miles multiplying.

Am I a coward? Is it cowardice to refuse to keep in shape—such a meaningful phrase—twelve long, incessant, successive months a year? Who can do it? Who can bear the gray ships? Dozens of them are running aground at this moment, hundreds of shipwrecks, hundreds of heads crossed out, slashed by a red felt-tip pen.

"Give me a little time," I asked, but you were taking your oversize, three-quarter-length coat down from the stand. Just a few weeks, my injured lady, but you were already yielding to velocity.

I suppose that Brezo had guessed I would rush out the door, try to beat the elevator by taking the stairs to reach it at the bottom. She must have stopped in a doorway or, who knows, waited silently on one of the landings. Her mind would not be changed. She had decided never to see me again.

How futile, Sergio and his shirt, Sergio and his shoes searching for her at eleven in the morning. I was dizzy from lack of sleep. The racket in the plaza deafened me. Passersby, pushing and shoving, invited me to dance. A woman walked by on the other side of the street in elegant high heels, a cluster of thistles in her hand. I remembered the beginning of a poem I had learned in high school: "It is not man who rests but his suit." One of my desires is to forget about Sergio, to just be my suit. To stay on a chair: a pair of pants folded over the seat of the chair, a jacket hung on the back, an unknotted tie while Sergio lies panting in his dreams. But there would be no rest. To go to sleep now, I told myself, would be to give reality a generous lead of several hours. I stopped twice for coffee, then went into the Archaeological Museum. A discreet cathedral, high ceilings, the distant sound of footsteps, space in which to collect myself and make a decision. Brezo, smoke of the incense high in the naves, flooded plexus, smoldering resin of your hair, don't leave.

I discovered a bench with two chairs hidden in a nook. My eyes shut, I remembered that you had returned. It was my dream, my god, and it was true. You did come, placed your body in my hands, whispering, "Make me weak in the knees." You crossed the city to speak your last two words: Let's go. But Sergio hesitates. You entered my house to stay, and I, who am dying, oh yes, dying for a piece of you, I, who would kiss you four hundred times, am hesitating. I retreat, behold the sin I am committing. You are a gift, a gift in my bedroom, while I, the most negligent of creatures, waver. I am trembling because I have no place to stand. How, Brezo, can you be asking me to go with you? There are laws in love as well. The ripest of gestures will rot, the continuous sound becomes inaudible, and only when it suddenly stops do we hear the vanished note.

I shook my head to drive out your image, allowing that "you still might come." But it was difficult. By the niches where statues stood like bones a throng of children lingered. Then all of a sudden they invaded my sitting room, and it was a sign. They drove me to keep searching for the hollow in the fabric of an overcoat and beyond. A professor from Murcia, for example, had decided to bring his students to the Archaeological Museum on the last Friday of January, perhaps to push me from one hall to the next, to tell me, "Keep looking." With a world so full of presences, Brezo, if I pay attention to them, why not to you? Why not go with you to the ends of the Earth? Why wouldn't I want to confound you with the dubious end of all things?

54

I went to see Maravillas Gaia again. I was received by a nurse I hadn't seen before. Flowery cuffs peeked out from the white sleeves of her lab coat and the hem of a gauzy skirt that looked like a slip was visible below.

I dutifully answered all of her questions, but when her arm pointed to a frosted glass door instead of the psychologist's office, I took offence.

"Who are you?"

"My name is Conchi," she said, opening a hideous pair of glasses. "I'm the secretary."

"But you're wearing a nurse's coat."

"I like to work in uniform."

She had put on her glasses. They were quite large and made of fuchsia-colored plastic.

"Is this your first day?"

"I asked for a leave of absence and now I'm back. Do you have any other questions I could answer for you, Mr. Prim?"

Brezo, other people may enter life with a sufficiently thick membrane, a vertical margin in their notebook that provides them with the distance and security they need. Perhaps they don't have boundary issues. I do. There was no distance between the point where that woman spoke with irony and the point where I received it. I suddenly felt mistreated. I am like a small, retractile animal, lacking a membrane. That is why my heart clenches up: it is the cramping of an aching heart. You sense my pain, and that is why you have such a hard time dealing with me.

"Please tell the psychologist I can't wait," I said in a tiny, distressed voice. I went to the waiting room, wondering who would be there, what stories might lie sleeping in their hands flipping through magazines, but all I found were dark red vases with golden threads, glass cases, and cabinets.

A short while later the secretary very decorously came to get me. "Sergio Prim!" she called in a booming voice. Then, smiling, she said, "It's your turn."

Maravillas looked as if she had woken from a nightmare, her desktop had expanded, and the armchairs were lower than ever.

"What's the news, Mr. Prim?"

"I'm ready to go into action and I need to do it now."

"Calm down," she said, but her voice, fuzzy and remote, held no authority.

"No, I won't. Ask me questions, do with me what you will, but make it quick. I am running out of time and I still don't know how to alter space. Maravillas, reality is after me, reality is getting closer and closer. I'm afraid she might even take my memory."

The psychologist, Brezo, got upset with me.

"Mr. Prim," she said, "I too was mistaken in thinking my discoveries would be of use to me in living my life. You are a mirror in which I see the woman I once was. Please leave this office."

"But I'm still prepared to explore the hollow. I assure you that I will calm my nerves, do whatever I am told, so that you and your Polish colleagues can make use of me," I mumbled, unable to believe they were kicking me out, expelling me from class.

"The experience of a single subject is not meaningful."

"I thought I understood that I was subject number two, at least. There was also Julio Bernardo Silveria."

There might have been a moment of hesitation in the psychologist's blue eyes. Then she got up to walk me to the door.

"A couple of years ago, you and I would have made a good team. But we also would have done each other a great deal of harm. Trust me, Mr. Prim, one cannot lock oneself within a conviction as one might within a book."

"But that Portuguese man. . . . "

"Forget all that. I can't see you anymore. I need to speak with Elena Morales. I ask you, please, leave me alone."

I took a long look at her. Maravillas, I thought to myself, don't give up. If we publish this, if we spread the news of that slight curvature, that pause in space that doesn't always push us the way time does, if we can figure out how to multiply and extend this potent resting place of ours like vitamins, like antibiotics. But she was already turning her back on me.

Nevertheless, I left her office determined to substantiate the source of the hollow with proof. And all the while, you were in travel agencies, recalling my absence with incomprehension. You say, "He was adored and went into hiding. His devotion was a thing of beauty, his steady gaze never flinched, and he went into hiding. Prim was pursued, overtaken by his own dream, and he went into hiding." Because I tried to get you to sleep with me inside the colors of the light. I am learning that everything else was irrelevant: I am writing the second part of this for you, that possible, meticulous life. But come and sleep when evening arrives. May time not wake you, rather, may you wake it, here in this chamber of music. And then the winters will come, one after another. We must persist; it is important to adorn the coldest of abodes. But you haven't left. You accompany me like the slender, golden second hand inside my watch.

55

A woman visits various floors of several large department stores and to determines that they sell everything she isn't looking for. In the same fashion, I followed a map, traveling the pathways I came across until I made it to the office.

I placed my bets on the main entrance and when doña Elena came out I followed her. I couldn't decide where I should stop her to talk. That tree-filled plaza looked like a box full of leaves, but that's where she was heading. And when she got there:

"Doña Elena! Do you have a minute?"

Doña Elena was nice to me. She listened as she would to a foreigner fresh off the boat. She gave me my bearings, explained the currency, the time zone of that country. She didn't even say, "You're very nervous." She walked me around the plaza, her small feet navigating the amber of broken bottles. I talked on and on.

"Have you read Maravillas Gaia's dissertation? I want to know about it right now. Tell me, does it explain disappearances? What happened to the Portuguese guy? Were there numbers, formulae, were there proofs?"

She responded with irony.

"Numbers, as you certainly remember, are ways of denoting

the landscape. We can describe the height of a garden wall using height in yards or by comparing it to the height of a horse. Why are you focused on numbers, Sergio? What are you worried about?"

There are questions that are unaware of their awful content, their intent to provoke anguish. What was I worrying about? I was worried about you. But just as I was about to confess this, your eyes grew large like the jets of fountains, causing mine to glaze over. How could I say, "I am afraid, doña Elena, of losing the one I am avoiding. I am afraid that I don't know how to hide from the one I love the most"?

"Maravillas," I explained, "promised to help me in exchange for my helping her, and now it seems she is backtracking."

"Maravillas is a difficult person," doña Elena said, somewhat embarrassed. "When she began her dissertation, her personality changed. Shortly after she abandoned it, we stopped seeing each other." She stared at me. She was blushing and seemed to be trying to determine my own state of orphanhood, determining the extent to which I needed her words.

"I wouldn't want to say anything indiscreet," she went on. "I will just say, for I understand that you are experiencing a similar problem, that Maravillas has not yet found what she was looking for."

Doña Elena stopped walking. Water welled up and floated in her eyes.

"And I can't wait for her any longer."

Elena Morales was a hub in that plaza, the beams of radii converging on her slight shoulders and her elegant coat.

"I'm sorry but I have to go," this convalescing soul said apologetically. Then she took a breath. "Congratulations on your recent report," she said with uncommon tranquility.

I kissed her moonbeam hand and watched her walk away.

Great deeds, Brezo, had taken shape. The great deeds had been accomplished and all that remained now was surprise or death. I don't want to destroy you. I have studied the cold air of my hope. You will clap me on the back like the rain, will fall on the nape of my neck like the downpours of January, and I will want to die then and there because I am weak, because I am a somber, solitary individual who would pervert himself, spill himself over your body until he was undone, a trickle of blue liquid vanishing in the morning light. A severe case of pneumonia and my naked body turned into a puddle, my body stretched out on the damp, green grass—this is what I can offer you. And that, Brezo, is why I can't join in your dreams. That is why I flee happiness.

Doña Elena walked away down Callejón del Gato, but it was as if Brezo had come running to take her place. Brezo reigned in the radii without asking me for help. Leaves from a faded autumn caught in the hem of my mackintosh.

I entered a pub to have some more coffee, as if it were gin or some other kind of alcohol that could push me far from consciousness. Though I ordered a sandwich to help me walk the last few blocks, I would have preferred not to eat, not to utter a single word, to be the man who never acquires solidity, who leans against the corners of buildings, savoring his memories by himself, relishing that slowness your body used to give me, while an unstoppable, inextinguishable depth of sorrow tells me I am going to lose you, tells me that feelings fall like unfastened skirts.

A rain shower swept through the air, quick drops to polish the buds on the trees. The weekend approached, shiny and new, childhood's choo-choo train, and office workers and children, couples in love and old people in pale guayaberas all got on board. I stayed behind, didn't buy you a ticket, Brezo, so you might ride with me. Instead, I turned my back on the bustling thoroughfare, headed for Calle Príncipe, and went to the office. It was deserted, as it always was on Friday afternoons. Then Sergio Prim put his heart on a window crank and wrote: I would have liked to be a hero, to have been killed in Karakua Bay but not before having discovered the eastern coast of Australia like James Cook, to have drowned in the Niger like Mungo Park but only after having charted its course. I would like to leave, to vanish, but only after having determined the latitude of a name, its volcanoes and lakes, its many species of plants, its climate. I would like to have been the stellar example, the flare that was lit and then disappeared, revealing how the others burn.

I will tell you, dear readers, how I burned. I will tell you that since that last Friday in January my hands have not known another body but these vain and silent pages. Outside, revolutions are being made, czars are being installed and deposed, while I think of my Zembla and rapidly turn gray. I will tell you that I never said goodbye to Brezo, only to a voice abducted by the swell of pride. I will tell how I discovered that the Vanished One no longer waits for these unruly lines, and how, nevertheless, my manner of speaking still tends toward the second person, wants to tell you about a painting, *The Geographer*, by J. Vermeer. Do you remember it? A window bathes the shadowy room with light. The geographer leans over the unfolded map. At his back, one can see the globe perched atop the dresser. But what most holds our interest is the dim interior, at the center of which we glimpse the geographer's pale face. One might say that his face is illuminated by the light of the window, but if you look at the painting—and I am looking at it now—you can tell that the brightness of his face comes from distant latitudes, nascent, unobstructed latitudes that inhabit the geographer in his darkened room. The geographer spreads lakes of dawn across his desk. This is his treasure, and it is everything I am now going to give you, my friend.

At eight in the evening the cleaning ladies changed from their tight-fitting clothes into their blue uniforms. I greeted them as they entered but didn't move. First they went through the building, then they moved around my floor, my office, and then, once again, their tight-fitting knitted jackets, their flowery blouses. I heard their banter as they waited for the elevator. If only they hadn't seen me, if only when they came in they hadn't acknowledged my presence by lowering their voices. Ungainly figure who is always with me, where could the Portuguese knight have gone? Let him come mounted on his horse, I want to see him coming. Maravillas, my inclement psychologist, you who befuddled my mind with great hopes, come now because Sergio is still here, unable to leave space behind like one of those strands of barbed wire we slip past in our childhood, yet neither can he gallantly hold the wire down that Brezo might jump over it.

I looked up, looked for the crank, looked for help. Outside there was a new gust of rain and I felt its drops coming in to drown my melancholy. The crank did not relinquish its stubby metal character: it was once more a small, compact part that offered me no protection. Reality's high-heeled shoes clicked in the street. The actress had tightened her net, denying me even the tiniest region—a window catch, a section of glazed tile, a fragment of a shadow in which I had so often hidden. The piece of fabric from the coat of the man riding the bus is a piece of fabric from his coat. It isn't hollow, and you don't disappear when you stare at it.

You're a bad actress, I said, scolding her. I have looked at those pieces as often as that man who rubs Aladdin's lamps, waiting for space to open up and swallow me. Bad actress, those pieces look like the shard of lava a tourist picked up, proof of the day he spent on the volcano; they are spices transported from the Indies because the Indies exist. Bad actress, enough of solitude, enough of my feeling that I am with Brezo interfering with your job. Reality, I visited beds, houses, gardens with my beloved, and you were always there. But now I am going to penetrate curved space with her: together we will suffer a swoon of reason where thought recedes and suddenly there is no longer a subjugated reverie but a hollow, a controversy of air against air. I have learned that, like a network of railway lines, a weft of feelings exists. Secret lines connect my delicate emotions with Brezo's turbulent waist, that waist someone else may be kissing at this very moment. No matter. The hollow flees the currents of time, ignores the mail slots, the ill-timed messages on the answering machine. The hollow never demands a visit. The hollow only needs to know that during nights of insomnia prison cells and dwellings interweave, and that, over the course of the day, reverie passes through a honeycomb of floating rooms. Sergio Prim knocks silently and one afternoon he pushes the door and, resting in the back of the room, a cat sleeping on the sofa, is you, Vanished One, and you open your eyes and are happy to see me.

The night has seeped through the closed blinds: black room full of machines, the peaceful, mute shapes of computers, empty wastepaper baskets like wells at the corner of the tables. A surface emptied of meaning, so many offices with no one in them, so many uninhabited buildings—hollows—over the weekend in the city. I thought of us, all of us, velvet girls, men with heart murmurs. Listen to me, all of you. We are going to establish a parallel itinerary. In the morning, weak men and women will occupy the houses their inhabitants have left to go to work. At night, we will sleep in offices, in shuttered stores, in the great postal palaces, naves full of still packages. Weak men and women will inhabit the hollow developments on certain beaches in the winter, will listen to the radio in empty cars sitting in parking lots. Men and women with a parallel schedule. They would never allow it to happen.

A milky shadow appeared in the bedroom: the wind had uncovered the moon. I thought I saw scarlet willows under the window instead of black asphalt. The wind erased the moon and erased you, because you were leaving, because I would not be accompanying you. But I should at least express myself to you in writing, even if you, Brezo, are not the recipient of my folios—I know all too well how you loathe excuses—but you, my hidden, delicate cohort of introverts.

Swathed in the bluish light of an adjustable desk lamp, staring at the tiny lights of the computer, Sergio piloted the propeller plane you wouldn't be taking, oh, my vanished one. I pressed the keys to send the notes I had written over the previous months to the printer and went downstairs to clear my head, because there was a pain there, a noise in my temples, the heavy creaking of the train taking you away. When I returned, the printer could still be heard wailing, and life was like a stag, bellowing improbably inside a dark, uninhabited office building.

Furtive hunter that I am, I fled the next day. I escaped your nearly transparent eyes, left early, and came to lodge here at The Scarlet Ox, that fabricated animal, that deep region of my chest, that space rising above its ashes, above slow osier willows. In my briefcase were all my notes, and in my suitcase, wrapped in my padded mackintosh, was a bouquet of bills, symbol of my extravagance and my madness. There was no train this time, no taxi afterward, just a single, obsessive thought: when would I call you, Brezo, what disgraced and tender words would I employ to confess my infamy, my journey, unobstructed at last by the urgency of your body: Sergio Prim, alone on a steppe. See how he penetrates the thick of a forest when there is no longer any forest.

The boy with the cruel blue eyes collected my luggage while a certain bald man smiled, pleased by my request to stay until the end of April. The willows had not yet filled out with green, the last magenta tips swinging against the valley floor. I picked up the phone, but not to call you. Rather, it was to leave these words on the psychologist's answering machine: "Don't give up."

My piles of luggage were fossils beside my bed, the remnants of shells and carapaces. It seemed to me as if a prehistory of glaciers had seen fit to leave them there to seal a pact, to sign off on a destiny. And Sergio, whose hand still held the phone, lifted the receiver to his ear once more.

"Are you in Cuenca again?" you asked, disconcerting me.

"How did you know?"

"Someone saw you heading for the Atocha train station." Your voice sounded peaceful, sounded not sad. "You're calling to say goodbye, right?"

Like someone who illuminates a dark stairway with a cigarette lighter, you held out your words, a remedy for my awkward hesitation. But in the end you would get angry at me.

"How are you going to spend your time there, Sergio? What will you do?"

"I'm going to use it to search for a point that dissolves time, and then stay there. Others will come. Others will have to chart its latitude, its geography."

First I heard the apartment door close, then I heard the front door of the building slam shut, the sound of car horns, and I could make out the voice of the woman who announces flights and calls passengers in airports.

A wounded panther, an afternoon in June, now many years ago, you stood looking at the broad swaths of green grass at the Canal de Isabel II. This reminds me, you said, of the private school where I spent my summers. Your eyes filled with English horses, Brezo, and behind them I saw a library sheathed in wood, a tray with breakfast, orange marmalade, sun. I thought of saying to you: Make me a hollow in your past. The lost years of the other. But they don't belong to us. I will never know the raw material of your nostalgia, Sundays barricaded with songs, the face of your friend calling you on the phone. The past cannot be touched and the future is shrill: I will be mistaken, you will travel, she will pursue us, we will stumble.

I have been at The Scarlet Ox for forty days now. A week has passed since I got your letter telling me of a lingering love, a Basque jai alai player who had lived in the same dormitory as you in Helsinki and who now lives with you. Reality is so efficient, so industrious and vengeful, but she can no longer hurt me. Neither reality nor circumstances nor busybodies nor anyone else who might walk through the drawing room of The Ox nor the course life takes nor my limitations nor my mistakes nor misfortune nor time nor even you—not even you, Brezo In A Rush, not even you with all your contradictions—could smash the china shop of my dream, move the tiniest figure, alter the amazing story of Sergio Prim, what he did with your body when you would grow faint: you would tremble, my crazy one, and I would gather up your trembling. What is the difference between ten seconds and ten million years?

I stay in mostly. Occasionally I take a slow stroll around the plaza, occasionally I look at the valley from the church. I lunch with the other guests and then watch the nightly news. But I can skip the news for two or three days and know that this simple, premeditated gesture annoys reality. Because reality, as I've told you, is an actress, and my whimsy strains her. If, upon returning from my isolation,

I decide to strike up a conversation, there are short-circuits, for I am no longer contained in the vocabulary of others, I am not pondering the recent military confrontations or the train that derailed yesterday in Extremadura. Reality, Brezo, has crow's feet. She has ordinary innards and faded cheeks that the celluloid doesn't reveal. In short, her life depends on the projector, sounding like rain, on the dark theater, on the electrical current. And there are so many movie theaters, Brezo, it is highly unlikely that my images would overlap yours. Don't you see that when I say tree, I think of a Mediterranean pine while you picture firs? I say train and you hear the red, high-speed Talgo while I meant the old Lusitania Express. Amid this uncertainty, in the shadow of this profound strangeness, someone switches off the bewildering world outside. I stand back and your image spreads over me like an eyelid, and this, my friend, is more real than all our prickliness combined.

But problems, trivialities, have arisen. The other night at dinner, I had to endure a married couple, two nosy veterinarians. They wanted to know what I do. I am a reticent man, Brezo, but I don't know how to say no. As soon as I had finished explaining my project they launched their attack. Good heavens, reality, how vulgar your troops are. I tried to show them that the present is more than this parade of heavy bodies with their flesh and bones, cubes and spheres, liquids and solids. The present is above all subtle magma, shavings of the past mixed with future, image blended with feeling. Particles spin around, enveloping me, waves of the Vanished Woman's voice brush against me. I live within a pale and brilliant whirlwind. "I cannot prove that scientific truth must be conceived as a truth that is valid independent of humanity," said Albert Einstein. But that couple didn't know that abstract ideas are territories that have emerged, like painting, books, imagination. That couple was a pragmatic being with double-barreled deafening laughter and two pairs of fleshy hands. Its constituents, connoisseurs of puff pastries with dates and bacon, spoke to me of administrative procedures. "Have you asked for time off?" they asked me with a curiosity entirely lacking in respect, and "Do you think they'll save your job for you?" I took my leave and they must have said something to the bald man, for ever since he looks at me with suspicion. That same morning, when I went to extend my reservation for another month, he asked me to pay up front. I didn't even protest. Must I confess to him that certain matters no longer interest me? I've drawn the curtains, sunk into a comfortable darkness. Brezo, my friend, darkness is a right; let us demand it. I know arrogant people who go around asking for sun, who turn lightbulbs on in dark bedrooms. Tanned, youthful people. Let them live under the dazzling white spectrum of light, let them never hide, let them look at one another through magnifying glasses under fluorescent lamps, but they shall not deny me my darkness, my blurry shadows. For I want to live my life in black and white: silhouettes suggesting possible bodies, every possible body. I want to dwell in darkness so I can lick my scratches and scars, so I can tabulate data, figures, sparkles, outlines, fringes. I want, Brezo, the autonomy of dusk. My room grows cloudy. The blurry outline of my hand is bordered by its shadow advancing in the dim light, blending with the waxing darkness that seems endless.

60

I have asked advice of the bald man regarding the best way to get a reverse mortgage on my apartment, as I haven't finished paying off the original mortgage, and the bank would surely follow me to Alnedo with its bills. He has refused to give me any advice, tells me I'm crazy. Of course he can't be sane either, which is why he is failing to promote his business, encouraging me instead to return to Madrid. He says it's crazy to borrow money against the mortgage on one's own apartment, so I explain that I don't want an apartment but a spot, because one can't always make the grade, because for some people it turns out to be extremely complicated. I also tell him that in some spots space curves as if someone had spread it with a putty knife. He listens but only wants to know my work address, asks for the phone numbers of relatives and references. One day I nearly gave him your address, distant woman, though it suddenly occurred to me that I wouldn't want to watch this Basque jai alai player's hands touching my written name. When all is said and done, it is a trivial detail that no longer hurts.

The time of sadness has been passing, Brezo, the pain growing less and less. I don't know whom to thank. I don't know what might have happened were the pain to remain constant. If your presence had not continued to dwindle, I don't know how I would have been able to make it to this page. And this is a canticle. Can you hear it? Absent Brezo, speak to me of useless things. Tell me: was the hollow in vain? Was there any point in searching for it? Or was it pointless for me to dream of having you with me? Woman, as the hours trickle away I feel a chill of strawberries. I always hated strawberries, those pink pieces of gum, the dirty flavor of lollipops, yoghurt, and ice cream. I would dream of the freshness of the mint I was lacking that was you. The chill of mint always seems to be leaving, as if pushed away by the wind.

But I wouldn't want you to worry about me. I know perfectly well that the hollow isn't useless. If I lose my job I will try to live off it. I've considered writing to Professor Niewicz and proposing a series of lectures. I've heard of a British physicist, Paul Dirac, who did research into the existence of certain newly discovered particles: positrons or "*hollows* in a sea of negative energy." Perhaps he can put me in contact with his former students. And in the worst case, I can always make my home on a window crank. It is, as I've told you, just a question of scale. Facing the trapezoid formed by the wine reflected on the tablecloth, the scale of a man grows as the scale of the reflection decreases, producing a translucent pink field where the man can go and dwell. If you were to drop a piece of crust on an atlas opened to the map of the world, you would see, Brezo—quake, misplacement, dislocation of my soul—that it covers the same area as Denmark.

61

Oh, but there are those who boldly claim that Brezo never existed. I have proof, of course. Her scent irrefutably impregnates the edge of my lapels. But what do I have to prove? And what would I accomplish if I did? Has the difference between ideas of the senses and those of the imagination yet been determined? And if so, would you all be so kind as to tell me what it is? Explain how one can tell whether the understanding between two people, two souls, existed or whether it was simply a figment of the imagination. If, in fact, you deny that there is any difference at all, we agree. Go on and deny that I even exist. Do I exist or don't I? Do I exist or am I a creation of that woman in the high collar, the one sitting in the armchair she inherited from her grandparents when it all began? But what, what was it that began?

The bald man looks at me out of the corner of his eye. The pre-Raphaelite girl insists that I show her a photo of you. The denouement, Brezo, is imminent. One of these days when I come down to breakfast I will find her—red parasol, high heels—surrounded by suitcases and leather bags. She'll scan the reception room, looking for me. Sergio Prim has left, the walls, windows, and trees will tell her. Sergio disappeared one day, like the Soviet Union, like the GDR, the way movie theaters and feelings—I loved her, a voice says—disappear. There are cruel and terrible countries where dead people are called disappeared. Though reality looks around for me, Brezo, she will not find me. To hide oneself, I now see, one should pick the spot where no one would ever imagine hiding. To be like the purloined letter, to change the address on the envelope, the color of the stamps, to turn over while remaining in the letter box, in plain sight, in full view, right where no one would think of hiding. So I have been here since the first letter, have not moved at all. In the end, I shifted scales and came to rest in this illuminated polyhedron. Two hundred and twenty-one rectangular pages with printed inscriptions, and between each word, at the edge of each letter, an interval, a hollow. Lift your hand and watch space stop.

Belén Gopegui burst onto the Spanish literary scene in 1993, bowling over critics with her masterful debut, *La escala de los mapas* [*The Scale of Maps*], which was hailed as a masterpiece. It was awarded both the Tigre Juan and the Iberoamericano Santiago del Nuevo Extremo prizes. She has since published six more novels, stories and screenplays. This is her first translation into English. Gopegui lives in Madrid, her native city.

Mark Schafer is a translator of the works of many Latin American authors, including David Huerta, Virgilio Piñera, Gloria Gervitz, and Alberto Ruy Sánchez. Schafer has received numerous grants and awards for his translations, including two translation fellowships from the National Endowment for the Arts. He lives in Boston, where he is a lecturer in Spanish at the University of Massachusetts Boston and a visual artist who specializes in reassembling maps to produce completely new geographies. For more information, visit www.beforesaying.com.